Nikki Barrowclough was born in New Zealand. She moved to Sydney in 1978 and has spent extended periods living overseas with her partner, a Frenchman. She is a journalist for the *Good Weekend* magazine. This is her first novel.

Monsieur Frog

nikki barrowclough

TEXT PUBLISHING
MELBOURNE AUSTRALIA

The Text Publishing Company
171 La Trobe Street
Melbourne Victoria 3000
Australia

Copyright © Nikki Barrowclough 2000

All rights reserved. Without limiting the rights under copyright above, no part of this publication shall be reproduced, stored in or introduced into a retrieval system, or transmitted in any form or by any means (electronic, mechanical, photocopying, recording or otherwise), without the prior permission of both the copyright owner and the publisher of this book.

This edition published 2000

Printed and bound by Griffin Press
Designed by Chong Weng-Ho
Typeset in 11.5/16.4 Sabon by Midland Typesetters

National Library of Australia
Cataloguing-in-Publication data:

Barrowclough, Nikki.

Monsieur Frog.

ISBN 1 876485 60 4.

A823.4

This project has been assisted by the Commonwealth Government through the Australia Council, its arts funding and advisory body.

To Alain René

'This his han houtrage! The French ave nussing hin cermmern with the Hinglish! Heven their pubic air his different! Hanglo-Saxons ave the merst hinvasive pubic air I ave hever seen hin my life! It grows erl hover the place, without hany sense erf direction!'

Zoe raised an eyebrow. 'Who on earth is that?' she said to Madeleine, glancing towards the doors that led into the garden, from where this impassioned shout had just come.

'No wernder the Hinglish are erlways mowing their lerns!' the same voice bellowed, before Madeleine could answer.

The fruit bats pushing and shoving each other in the trees outside suddenly went quiet. It took a lot to silence fruit bats, Zoe thought. The unexpected stillness, that Friday evening in Sydney in the late summer of 1998, was like a particularly effective prologue. Zoe was big on prologues. She had written a rather fine one for her novel. Then she had rewritten it several times. Unfortunately, somewhere along the line, it had turned into an epilogue. Exactly how this had happened, she wasn't sure. She sighed. A breeze began blowing across the eastern suburbs from the harbour, and the light, already fading, deepened the city's terracotta rooftops.

Zoe had just arrived at Max and Madeleine's house in Edgecliff. She had taken a taxi from Elizabeth Bay, where she lived alone in a tiny flat with glimpses of the North Shore. Her days in the flat, however, were numbered. Developers had bought the building, and intended turning it into a boutique hotel. Her eviction notice had arrived the week before.

Before she left for Max and Madeleine's, Zoe had allowed herself a glass of whisky. Normally, she wasn't a big drinker, but she had read somewhere that serious writers drank whisky as their alcohol of choice. Joan Didion probably did, Marguerite Duras certainly did and Mikhail Bulgakov probably had as well. Bulgakov *looked* like a whisky drinker, Zoe had reasoned, after an intense examination of the cover of *Manuscripts*

Don't Burn. She had positioned the book on the spare pillow on her bed, so that Bulgakov was the first man she saw every morning. At one stage she had briefly replaced Bulgakov with Malraux, who also had a fascinating face, but you never heard Malraux's name around the inner-city cafes, whereas everyone was reading Bulgakov again. The problem was that Bulgakov was dead. Luckily, Mario Vargas Llosa was very much alive. The black catsuit with cut-away shoulders which Zoe wore to Max and Madeleine's was a Vargas Llosa-induced purchase.

'You've got whisky on your breath,' Madeleine remarked, running a critical eye over Zoe's new fringe, and the way she had twisted her hair up under a small black cap. 'What is this—the *Wild Swans: Three Daughters of China* look? You're extremely late, you know. Everyone else arrived an hour ago.'

'I think it's a very literary hairstyle,' retorted Zoe. 'The cap was just a whim. You've mistaken the look entirely. And I'm late because social obligations seem entirely irrelevant when you've been trying to reconceptualise a narrative for the fourth time in two days.'

Zoe was famous among her friends for the excuses she gave whenever she turned up late at their parties. 'You have no idea how deeply problematic the notion of character is in post-millennial fiction, since my book won't be ready to be published before then. It took

Proust years, as well,' she was pointing out to a resigned-looking Madeleine, when the demented shouting started up again from the garden.

Zoe walked outside to the top of the steps. She peered down at the group of people posed beneath the grove of palms, whose slender trunks and brilliant green fronds had so thrilled her when Max and Madeleine first bought the house. 'Doesn't it remind you of Somerset Maugham in Malaya?' she had breathed at the time.

'That's the owner of the accent there,' said Madeleine, joining her on the steps, and pointing at a tall man in his forties with untidy, light-brown hair (of the non salon kind), a large Gallic nose and an imperious demeanour. He alone among the guests had not bothered to dress up for Max and Madeleine's dinner party, and was wearing a badly ironed, blue-striped shirt, which showed the beginnings of a belly, blue jeans, a red cotton jumper slung casually around his shoulders, and a pair of faded, blue and red leather boat-shoes.

'Max met him in a bar in Paris when he was on holiday there years ago,' Madeleine continued, 'and they've been close friends ever since. He appeared from out of the blue a few months ago and says he's here for good.'

Zoe studied the animated figure who was monopolising everyone's attention. He had a glass of champagne in one hand, a cigarette in the other and seemed oblivious to the fact that he kept flicking ash over an anorexic redhead with violet eyes standing close by. The couple he had been shouting at turned their backs on him, and began comforting a little girl who was cowering behind their legs.

'He's far from being your Yves Montand type, I know,' remarked Madeleine, looking every inch a banker's wife with her expensively beaded strapless 'corset' top, pearls and jewel-encrusted watch. People always did a double take when they met her for the first time. The biting business column she wrote each week for the *Australian Financial Review*, gave people an entirely different impression. 'But he can be extremely charming when he wants.'

'Really?' said Zoe doubtfully. She looked back towards the group, where someone else—it was Louise, she noticed, a colleague of Max's, whom she knew—had taken over the conversation.

'You'd think a Frenchman would dress a bit better,' Zoe commented, wondering briefly who the anorexic redhead was. 'How old is he?'

'Forty-six, nine years older than you.'

'I hope he's not called Pierre,' said Zoe, ignoring this reference to her age—a sensitive subject, and one becoming increasingly so, as more and more books by other, much younger writers, kept appearing on the market. 'Pierre is *such* a cliche, in literary terms,' she added.

'No, he's not called Pierre. He's called something worse,' Madeleine replied. 'I prefer to call him Le Grand Alain. As you can see, he enjoys his food and drink. I also call him that because it sounds so much better than the Frog, which is what Max started calling him after watching him eat frogs' legs at dinner one night. Apparently, he ate so many that the restaurant put up a plaque in his honour. Since then, everyone knows him as "the Frog". It's become his title. I even saw it on a wedding invitation in his flat in Paris, once. Come on,' she said, taking Zoe's arm, 'I'll introduce you before he causes any more diplomatic incidents.'

As the two women walked down the steps, the Frenchman in the garden went berserk again. 'It merst ave been the garlic!' he shouted, clasping a hand to his chest. 'Wert a magnificernt death! Vive la France!' And he began to bawl 'The Marseillaise'.

The fruit bats had had enough. They rose from the trees screeching and flew off towards Bellevue Hill.

'What's going on?' Madeleine asked Max, who had detached himself from the guests to greet Zoe.

'Louise was telling us about a story that was on the news the other night,' said Max, a gnomish-looking man with long, fine fingers and beautiful half-moons. 'An elderly woman in the west of France spontaneously combusted. That's the theory the authorities came up with in the end, because there was nothing left of her except a pair of spectacles and a sock.'

'And your friend from Paris thinks garlic caused her to explode?' Zoe snorted. 'He's joking, surely!'

'I'm afraid not,' Max replied. 'You have to understand the Frog's particular slant on life. To him, it could only have been garlic that caused the old lady's spontaneous combustion. He regards her death as a tribute to one of the greatest mainstays of French cooking.'

'The day erl my bits and pieces start ferlling erf, I wernt to blew herp hin hexactly the same manner!' the Frenchman was proclaiming as they joined the group. 'They'll prerbably stert ferlling erf hany day now,' he added morosely.

As well as Louise, Zoe knew three of the other guests including Russell, Louise's current lover. Russell was an artist who had won the previous year's Archibald Prize amid controversy, with a portrait of his biggest rival in the art world poking a paintbrush through his eye— apparently in an act of self-mutilation. She also knew Eva, a blonde, obsessive German-born fitness instructor who was Madeleine's personal trainer, and Howard, an eminent psychiatrist, who looked like James Joyce with a beard, Zoe had always thought with approval, and who was forever on the prowl for hopelessly confused women.

'This is Antarctica,' Howard said immediately, introducing Zoe to his latest find, the bony redhead. 'Her mother was born in Darwin and spent her entire life dreaming of living somewhere cold.'

'She had an obsession with snow and ice,' said Antarctica in a husky voice.

'Like Smilla,' Zoe remarked.

'Who?' Antarctica asked.

'Never mind,' said Zoe, making a mental note—*she doesn't read*.

'Tell me,' she went on, 'did your mother ever visit Antarctica itself?'

'No. She didn't want to frighten the penguins. She hated all those scientific expeditions. "They'll scare the penguins," she used to say.'

'Antarctica is sponsoring a penguin in the zoo in memory of her mother,' explained Howard. 'She makes a pilgrimage to see her penguin every Tuesday. It brings her peace of mind.'

'Wert a waste erf time,' barked a rude voice on Zoe's left. 'You are nert herllowed to heat penguins, so why berther?'

There was a sharp intake of breath from the couple Zoe hadn't met, the ones the Frog had been shouting at. They were still standing in the same position as before, slightly removed from the rest of the group, keeping a protective eye on the little girl who had seemed so upset.

On the stone bench next to her, as Zoe saw now, there was a baby fast asleep in a papoose.

'This is Donald and Judith Fitzwimpleton, who have bought the house next door to us,' said Madeleine. 'And that's Donald Junior in the papoose, and his sister, Daisy, who's four.' The little girl whimpered and clutched her mother's cream acetate polyester trousers. 'The Fitzwimpletons are management consultants. They run one of the biggest management consultancies in the country.'

'We specialise in attitudinal objectives,' said Donald Fitzwimpleton, a shiny, well-groomed man with gelled brown hair, who spoke in polished, well-articulated tones. 'Don't we, Judith?'

Judith Fitzwimpleton, equally gelled and well groomed, in a cream silk shirt with a pointed collar, smiled briefly but did not reply.

'And this, of course, is Le Grand Alain,' said Madeleine, without losing a beat, 'about whom you have heard so much already.'

'Ave you really? I am so very flertted,' said the Frenchman, raising Zoe's hand to his lips and kissing her fingers. He had intense blue eyes. 'You ave wernderfurl shurlders,' he remarked, walking around her and studying her, Zoe thought, as if he was Rodin contemplating a half-finished sculpture—an idea that rather appealed to her. 'Hand I like lerng legs very merch. Hand you ave a very nice berk.'

'My…? Oh, you mean my back. How…flattering.'

'Are you lerking fur a lerver?'

'A what? Oh—no, I'm not.'

'Hin Paris, wormen are erlways lerking fur lervers.'

'This isn't Paris. I'm not looking for a lover. I'm here because I was invited by Max and Madeleine, who are old friends of mine.'

The Frenchman continued to gaze at her. 'Do you like pigs' trertters?'

'I've never eaten them,' said Zoe, on firmer ground, 'and I never will.'

'Non? Why nert?'

'I refuse to eat the feet of murdered pigs. They're extremely intelligent animals. Voltaire knew that. Pigs *hate* being murdered.'

'Dern't we erl,' the Frog replied lugubriously, and lit a cigarette.

Zoe coughed and batted the cigarette smoke away from her. Mikhail Bulgakov had also smoked—but even so. 'You're very tall for a Frenchman,' she remarked.

This was probably the worst thing she could have said.

'Wert do you mean? You sink we are erl smerll, with berets ern our eads?'

The outrage in his voice alarmed her. 'I'm sorry, it's just that—'

'We were erl as terl as ouses, wernce,' he carried on,

talking over her. 'Bert erl the terll men went erf to fight hin the Napoleonic Wars and they nevaire returned. A terriberl scandal! I sink I ham the ernly true Frenchman left. You ave a very sexy berm,' he went on without drawing breath, accepting a glass of red wine from Max. 'Berms erlways remind me erf capsicerms. I like capsicerms very merch.'

'Zoe's a writer,' Max interjected, as Judith Fitzwimpleton glared. 'She's been writing a novel for the past six years, but she won't let anyone read it. She won't even tell us what it's about.'

'What *is* the plot, Zoe?' Louise asked.

Zoe, who hated being questioned about her novel, especially since it kept changing all the time, decided on the spur of the moment that perhaps she *should* shed some light on the subject matter. Perhaps as a result, she'd understand it better herself.

'There is no plot,' she said. 'The plot-driven novel is a very old-fashioned concept and an inferior, literary construct. As a result, my book is more intellectually driven. While it takes novelistic liberties with the pursuit of aesthetic principles and motives, it is not a novel in any conventional sense. However, it still recognises that the infinite navigation between the narrative voice and the banality of the real, will, in the end, tell the story.'

'That's very impressive,' said Donald Fitzwimpleton, looking at Zoe with new respect.

No one else said anything. As the silence became embarrassing, Madeleine gave Max a nudge. Max cleared his throat. 'So what's the title?' he asked.

'I'm still investigating the possibility of contemplating a title,' Zoe answered.

'You mean you haven't got one,' said Russell. 'It sounds to me as if you're not getting very far with the novel at all. Why don't you write my biography instead? I've always wanted to be a literary event.'

'A good idea! Literary biographies are very trendy,' agreed Eva, who had hung out at the last Sydney Writers' Festival in the hope of giving Paul Theroux a workout, and had picked up a few valuable pointers.

To Zoe's surprise, the Frog, who had been following this conversation with a perplexed look on his face, came to her defence. 'You sherd nevaire make fun erf horsers,' he admonished everyone. 'Horsers are very mishernderstered.'

'I think you mean "authors",' said Madeleine.

'Oui, that's hexactly wert I said. Horsers ave to sit very still fur hours. Erl my life I werndered, "Wert's their secret?" Then, wern day, I ferned hout the answer. They furget to heat. That's why they take so lerng to write their noverls. Years and years. Becurse they are sterving to death. They ave no henergy to move, let erlone write. So when they go to the cafe they ferll hover.'

'I'm afraid it's been years since I read Sartre,' Zoe said nervously, trying to remember whether the founder of French existentialism had ever fallen over at Deux Magots. She assumed that was who he was talking about. The French always talked about Sartre, didn't they?

'Bouf! Sartre his hirrelevant,' the Frog replied. 'Bert Camus his hanerther matter. E used to heat leek soup when e wers writing *L'Etranger*. Nert many people know habout this link between leeks hand literature. Do you make leek soup, Zoe?'

'I'm afraid I can never remember which end of a leek is which,' Zoe admitted.

'Surely you are jerking,' the Frog replied, aghast, dropping his cigarette and staring at her as if she came from another planet. 'Merde alors! Sermsing merst be dern habout this catastrophe himmediately! I ave the solution. I merst hinvite you fur dinner termerrow night.'

Zoe opened her mouth to decline. 'I'd love to,' she said instead.

'Bon! The first curse will be leek soup, to elp you becerm mere like Camus. Then I will sterff serm quails with serltanas, bacern, honions and cous-cous, and roast them hin the hervern. My quails are a leetle miracle. Heverywern says so.'

'Leek soup in summer?' Louise asked. 'Isn't that the wrong season?'

'Dern't be ridiculers,' replied the Frog. 'Sermmer, winter, hauterm, spring—wert is the difference? Leek soup sherd erlways be hexploited!'

'You're obviously very big on leek soup,' remarked Russell, who wasn't. 'I prefer food that's more surreal.'

'Leek soup is my spiritual connection to la France profonde!' the Frog responded, which shut Russell up.

The Frenchman turned back to Zoe. 'Or werd you prefer that I cerk poussins hin tarragern serce with leetle potatoes hin goose fat, or spertchcerk with petit pois?'

'You seem to like eating small birds,' Antarctica said at this point.

'Herf curse! Wert helse are they fur?'

Antarctica made a fluttering movement. 'You should make a large donation to the RSPCA,' she said.

'Mais, pourquoi?' asked the Frog, astonished.

'It's very kind of you to invite me to dinner,' Zoe interrupted. 'But there's no need to go to any trouble. I'm quite happy to have a toasted sandwich.'

Time stood still.

'I will pretend you nevaire made that desgersting remark, Zoe,' said the Frog, once he had taken his face out of his hands. 'But vraiment!' he blurted a second later, 'honly han Hanglo-Saxon cerd say serch han houtrageous sing!'

Max clapped his old friend on the back and winked at Zoe. 'You had better be careful if you want to make a good impression. Zoe judges people solely on what they read—not on what they eat.'

Le Grand Alain, astounded by this revelation, lit another cigarette. 'The lerst berk I read wers by Charles Bukowski—the greatest writer hin the world after Rabelais and Montaigne. Rabelais wrote magnificently about cuisine. Ave you read *The Eroic Deeds herf Gargantua and Pantagruel*? I know ole passerges erf that mersterpiece by art.' Putting down his wineglass, he closed his eyes and his expression grew dreamy.

'E cermbed is air with an altman cermb, which is the four fingers and the thermb,' the Frog began to quote. 'For his perceptor said, that to cermb himself hin erther ways, to wersh and make himself neat, wers to lerse time hin this world. Then e dernged, pissed, spuked, belched, cracked, yawned, spitted, cerffed, yexed, sneezed, and snertted himself like an arc-deacon, and to suppress the dew and bad air, went to breakfast, aving serm good fried tripe, fair rashers hon the coals, hexcellent gammerns herf bacern, a store erf fine minced meat...'

Zoe suddenly became aware that tears were streaming down the Frenchman's face. 'Don't worry,' Max reassured her. 'He always gets emotional when he quotes from *Gargantua and Pantagruel*.'

'It's serch beautiful writing,' the Frog snuffled. 'Sermtimes I sink Gargantua is my spiritual twin.'

'I'm afraid I haven't read much Rabelais,' said Zoe. 'And Bukowski—doesn't he drink too much?'

'Bert herf curse Bukowski drinks!' roared Le Grand Alain. 'E's a writer! This is wert writers do! It's hin their blerd! I werd like ter be a writer very merch, but it's himperssiberl, becers I cerd nert bear to be so angry erl the time. Is your father a writer too, Zoe?'

'My father is a doctor,' Zoe replied, trying to work out why the Frog thought writers were always angry.

'This his hexcellent news!' cried the Frenchman. 'I merst make an happointment to see im right away!'

'The French,' Eva interrupted, 'are the biggest hypochondriacs on earth, not like we Germans. I myself am a particularly healthy example of the motherland!'

To everyone's bemusement, she dropped to the ground and began to do a series of push-ups.

'My father is a gynaecologist,' Zoe told the Frog, trying to distract him from Eva's performance, as well as her derriere.

'So wert? E werd still recergnise leprosy, werdn't e?'

'What on earth are you talking about?' asked Howard.

'My herm. It's a ferny cerleur. I sink hit's leprosy. I ad a medical checkherp at the herspiterl yesterday—I ave them twice a week—bert my specialist said hit's honly a beetroot stain.'

The Frog rolled up his sleeve as he spoke, and everyone leaned forward. There were a couple of maroon coloured splotches just above his wrist.

'It *is* beetroot,' said Howard.

'I do nert believe you!' fumed the Frog. 'I ave a disease you dern't recergnise, that's erl.'

'Perhaps you should wash more,' suggested Donald Fitzwimpleton. 'Everyone knows the French bathe only once or twice a week.'

'Bouf!' the Frog retorted. 'Hanglo-Saxons wersh too merch. That's why they erlways smell herf serp. Why do you lerk so cernfused, Zoe?'

'It's just that sometimes you add an "h" to your words and sometimes you don't, and I can't predict when you're going to,' she replied.

'I ham very hernpredictaberl, Zoe.'

Eva got back to her feet and after jumping up and down on the spot ten times remarked to Zoe, 'I still don't understand why it's taking you so long to write this book. Your circulation is probably too sluggish.'

'I bet no one ever suggested to Tolstoy that his circulation was sluggish,' Zoe answered. 'Or Proust. And I can assure you, there's nothing sluggish about trying to write like Proust.'

'Why don't you try to write like Helen Fielding?' asked Louise, who was a fan. 'Then you could write things like, "Why don't you just go fucking fuck yourself?" which is my favourite Bridget Jones line of all time.'

'Oh please!' Judith Fitzwimpleton remonstrated. 'There are children present!'

On cue, little Daisy burst into tears. 'I want my guinea pig!' she wailed, grinding her fists into her eyes.

Throwing a furious look at the Frog, Judith Fitzwimpleton scooped up both her children and stormed back up the steps to the house. 'Max, you take over here,' said Madeleine. 'I'll go and help Judith.' She hurried off, followed seconds later by an equally grim Donald Fitzwimpleton.

'Bouf!' said the Frog. 'The Pisswomples ave no sense herf umour.'

'It wasn't something you said, by any chance?' Zoe inquired, batting his cigarette smoke away from her again.

'I merely asked them wert wers wreng with their baby,' the Frenchman shrugged. 'I said I sought there merst be sermsing wreng with im, becurse e lerked so ergly. I said that wrapped herp in erl those white blernkets, e lerked like a piece of bacern, ready to heat.'

Zoe looked at him in horror. 'How could you say such an awful thing? And what about the little girl?'

'She had er hidiotic pet guinea pig with er. I ave a simple philosophy hin life. If hit moves, heat it. When I said the guinea pig lerked nice and juicy, she became hystericerl. Max said I wers honly joking, bert I said I wersn't. I sink childrens sherd be terld the truth.'

'The guinea pig had to be taken back next door,' Antarctica explained. Zoe, still looking askance at the Frog, remarked, 'So you don't like children?'

'Hon the contrary,' the Frog replied. 'I like childrens very merch. I simply dern't hundersternd the hegotistical hinsistence to reproduce, hernless people ave perfect genes. The world is orriberl henerf herlready, without childrens being ferced to ave hadditionerl andicaps. Lerk at me. I ham a perfect hexamperl. I ave huge feets and a big nerse. I tried to hexplain this to the Pisswomples, bert naturally, being Hanglo-Saxons, they took heverysing I said has han hinserlt. Hanyway, heven if I didn't ave huge feets and a big nerse, I werd still ave no desire to reproduce myself,' he added. 'That werd be too depressing, dern't you sink?'

Antarctica had been listening to all this with a concerned expression, and said solicitously, 'You really should be in therapy. You obviously suffered some kind of terrible damage in your childhood.'

'I wers damaged by being bern!' roared the Frog.

'I understand you're confused—so am I, deeply—but somehow you have to convince yourself there's something to look forward to in life,' Antarctica insisted.

'There's nussing to lerk ferward to.'

'What about humanity's achievements?' Eva asked.

'Great moments in science and medicine. Low-salt butter.'

'I will pretend I didn't ear you mention that hatrocity,' the Frog replied.

'How about your childhood?' tried Howard.

'It wers very miserable. There wers herlways a werm hin my berthwater.'

'Berthwater?' queried Louise.

'I think he means "bathwater",' Howard replied.

'Hand then there wers the village concert,' the Frog continued, oblivious to any interruptions. 'I wers seven years erld, hand I wers going to be the greatest trempert-player hin the world. Bert when I sterd erp at the village concert to perferm my solo, my trermpert felled to pieces. My art broke, and I knew then that I wers cursed.'

'I said you needed therapy,' said Antarctica. 'You're obviously suffering from repressed memory syndrome caused from stimulus entrapment.'

'I do wish you'd stop reading my psychiatry books,' said Howard. 'You confuse everything, you know.'

'You are a shrank?' the Frog inquired politely. 'My cernderlences.'

'Not at all,' replied Howard. 'You never know, I may be of some use to you.'

'Mais non. There's no ope for me. I ham doomed.'

'Surely things aren't that bad,' said Zoe, feeling sorry

for this very odd man, as his face folded into the kind of expression which might be titled, 'Misery throughout the Ages', if captured in a portrait. 'Perhaps you've got some optimistic genes you never knew about.'

'Sank you Zoe, bert there's wern preblerm I can nevaire hescape from. I ham *erlways* angry.'

'Then you must learn to calm down,' said Zoe.

'Non, non, *angry*,' the Frenchman repeated, lighting yet another cigarette. 'Hit's a terrible haffliction, erlways to be so angry. I can nevaire, hever, sterp sinking habout food. In fact, erl my life, I ave been sterving to death. Bert if you werd ave sex with me, Zoe, sings werd change. I werd becerm as appy as Lerence.'

'Larry,' Howard murmured.

Zoe, furious at herself for falling for the Frog's act—putting himself forward as someone who cared deeply for literature and for writers, when he was obviously just another enterprising sex maniac with a foreign accent—deliberately turned away and asked Eva the best place to buy an exercise bike.

'Oui, hexercise his a good idea,' the Frog interrupted. 'Wern erf these days I merst try serm hexercise myself.'

'Do you mind?' said Zoe. 'I'm trying to have a conversation with Eva.'

'I wers terking to you first,' said the Frog, looking sulky. 'Hanglo-Saxons ave no idea ow to cernderct a cernversation. Zoe? Are you listening? Zoe! This his houtrageous! You ave hinserlted me beyernd reasern! I refuse to remain ere a moment lernger.'

Seizing an unopened bottle of wine from the garden table, he turned and stalked up the steps—ignoring Max's pleas for him to return.

*E*va, oblivious to the drama she had helped create, lay down on the ground and began demonstrating to Zoe the right way to ride an exercise bike. 'Come on, Zoe, writers need to improve their circulation! ' she cried, her legs pumping up and down. 'Bankers too! And artists! ' She was still exhorting everyone to join her in her virtual bike ride, when Madeleine, accompanied by the Fitzwimpletons, returned to the garden.

'Max,' said Madeleine, 'I can't find the trout. Where did you put it?'

'In the fridge of course,' Max answered.

'Well, it's vanished,' Madeleine fretted. 'And it was

meant to be the first course.'

'It's not the only thing that has vanished,' commented Russell. 'Your amusing French friend has disappeared as well. He reacted badly to Zoe giving him the cold shoulder. Perhaps there's a connection.'

'For God's sake,' said Zoe. 'I'm not the Frog's keeper. Can't I talk to anyone else around here?'

Madeleine looked at her. 'Come with me, Zoe,' she ordered. 'I don't think you realise what you've done.' As Zoe looked exasperated, she gripped her friend firmly by the arm.

'What happened exactly?' Madeleine asked, once the two of them were inside the house.

'He propositioned me in the crassest manner,' Zoe answered. 'I don't think he gives a fig for literature. Frenchmen will say anything to have sex.'

'Well, we have to find him, fast,' said Madeleine. 'I've just finished helping the Fitzwimpletons put their children to bed in Max's study downstairs. I said they should sleep in the spare bedroom upstairs, but Judith thought that was too far away for safety. If she discovers the Frog is on the loose, she'll call the cops. More importantly, I need him to help me cook the trout. And to give me some advice about lamb and flageolet beans. It's a classic French dish, and one of his favourites. God help me if I get it wrong.'

The two women set about finding the missing Frenchman, checking all the rooms downstairs, before going upstairs to continue the search.

'I don't understand it,' Madeleine said. 'Where could he have got to?'

At the far end of the hall, they heard the pop of a wine cork.

'He's in the spare bathroom!' Madeleine cried in relief. 'Go and get him! I have to check the lamb.'

'I am *not* going into the bathroom,' Zoe argued.

'You don't have to. Just knock on the door and tell him I need him.'

Zoe knocked on the bathroom door. No answer. She wiggled the door handle. It was locked. 'Look,' she said. 'I know you're in there, sulking. Personally, I couldn't care less. But Madeleine needs you. She thinks she's incapable of cooking dinner without your help, though I'm sure the lamb and flageolet beans are fine on their own. No one should take food that seriously. Literature, on the other hand, has real gravitas. You can't disguise the lumpy bits in your writing, by pushing them through a sieve and turning them into puree.'

No answer.

'So how long do you plan to stay in there?' she carried on.

'You hexpect me to rehemerge hin society has hif nussing has appened, hafter that hinserlting speech you jerst made?'

'Well, Madeleine needs you,' Zoe repeated. 'The trout has gone missing. You haven't seen it by any chance?'

'The trout is hin the bath with me. I ad nowern helse to keep me cermpany.'

Zoe, incredulous, absorbed this news, then marched downstairs where she found Madeleine in the architecturally hysterical kitchen, all stainless steel, designer lighting and invisible cupboard doors, knocking back brandy straight from the bottle. 'I think Howard should have him committed. He's in the bloody bath with the trout.'

'Oh no,' moaned Madeleine. 'What am I going to do?' She began frantically searching the fridge for something else to cook, when they heard the noise of water gurgling through the pipes upstairs. The sound went on for ages. 'We must do something about those pipes,' Madeleine muttered. 'A fortune's been spent on this place, and you can still hear that ridiculous gurgling when someone pulls the bathplug out.'

'I think Monsieur Frog pulled the bathplug, metaphorically speaking, a long time ago,' Zoe remarked.

A few minutes later the subject of their conversation arrived in the kitchen with a towel draped around his hips. 'I had to wersh my leetle feesh,' he explained. 'I pert too merch berth-hoil hin the berth. E's hokay now, I sink.'

'Thank God,' said Madeleine. 'Max has gone to start rounding everyone up for dinner. They must be starving. Tell me how you're going to cook the trout.'

'Very fast, hat terp speed, then very slow, then I will finish hit herf with lemon, parsley and buttaire,' said the Frog. 'My trout will be a leetle mersterpiece!'

'Nice to see you've calmed down,' Zoe commented, 'after your tantrum.'

'I ham erlways calm, Zoe,' the Frog rebuked her. 'It's herther people who are nevaire calm. Besides, now that I ham hin the kitchen, I dern't feel so lernly. The kitchen his the centre erf the huniverse, and food his the ernly noberl sing hin a world that is rottern to the core.' He knotted the towel tighter around his hips, and grabbed a frying pan. 'Where is the red wine? I need a glass erf red wine while I cerk!'

As Madeleine opened a bottle, Zoe left the kitchen and went into the dining room, where floor-to-ceiling windows looked across the rooftops to the harbour. As she stood there, the last of the light vanished like a thin swirl of silk, and Max, who had followed her into the dining room, turned on the lamps.

The dining room's red walls were hung with several paintings, including one by Norman Lindsay. Judith Fitzwimpleton flinched when she walked in and saw it. She sat down with her back to the voluptuous nude, before realising that she was now sitting opposite a life-sized sculpture of a female torso on a stand.

The others stood around the room talking, but were sent rushing to the table by a bellow from the kitchen. 'I wernt heverywern hat the table now! Hanglo-Saxons can nevaire be ern time! They sink food jerst grows ern plates!'

The guests whirled about, their social skills utterly askew, bumping into one another in their panic to seat themselves.

'Hokay? Ere we go!' came another battle cry from the kitchen, and then the Frog raced into the dining room, still wrapped in the bath towel, tendrils of hair sticking up on his head, a tea towel slung over one shoulder. He was holding two plates of trout. He deposited one of these plates in front of Zoe, then sat down next to her with the other one and started eating. Madeleine and Max, meanwhile, hurried around serving their other guests.

'Heat herp! Heat herp!' ordered the Frog. 'Dern't jerst stare hat your food!'

'It's polite to wait until everyone is served,' Judith Fitzwimpleton pointed out, blinking at the Frog's seminudity.

'Honly Hanglo-Saxons let their food go cold!' the Frog retorted.

'Don't you think you could have got dressed for dinner?' Donald Fitzwimpleton inquired in a cutting voice.

'I dern't like to be persecuted by my clothes,' came the answer.

Pointedly, Zoe handed the Frog his napkin, averting her eyes from the part of his belly that was poking over his towel.

'Sanks,' he said, replacing the napkin on the table. 'I prefur to use a tea twirl.' And he took the tea towel from his shoulder and tied it, like a bib, around his neck.

Zoe sighed, and imagined Mario Vargas Llosa in a dinner suit.

'Do you like my leetle trout, Zoe?' the Frog asked her, the minute she started eating.

'It's very good,' she admitted. 'And I can't taste any bath oil at all.'

'My trout is a miracle,' the Frog corrected her. Knocking his knife against his wineglass until he had everyone's attention, he proceeded to expand on the merits of his cooking as opposed to the pretentious, piss-arty, over-priced meals served in restaurants. This was before he started on the Napoleonic Wars. And well after he had finished eating.

'I don't think I've ever seen anyone bolt their food so fast in my life,' commented Louise, once the Frog came to the end of his lecture. 'You'd think it was your last meal on earth.'

'Ow do I know that it hisn't?' the Frog shouted. 'I ham hamerngst fureigners. Hanysing cerd appen!'

'Nonsense,' said Madeleine. 'The next course is lamb and flageolet beans, and I followed your instructions to the letter. I'm sure you'll be safe.'

'What's so special about flageolet beans?' Zoe asked, as Madeleine and Max began to clear away the plates.

'Flageolet beans, like gherkins, goose fat, petit pois and pigs' trertters, are to cerking wert the Mona Lisa his to the Louvre,' replied the Frog. He was wearing his imperious expression again. 'When I wers a child, living with my grandparents hin the French countryside, I used to play with hempty cans erf flageolet beans, which I pulled halerng ern a string.'

'I see,' said Zoe. 'So why did you leave France and all those cherished memories behind?'

'I had to leave!' snapped the Frog. 'Sermwern served me a frozen cassoulet hin a restaurant. Houtrageous! You nevaire, hever, freeze a cassoulet. Paris his going to the dergs! I perked my bergs and left soon hafter.'

'But you'll miss France after a while, won't you?' Zoe persisted.

'I will miss les brochets, the leetle feesh we used to find hin the Loire. My grandmerther taught me ow to cerk them hin white buttaire. Bert they erl disappeared from the Loire a lerng time ago. France is nert the same has it used to be.'

'Joseph Brodsky once wrote that you can't return to a country that doesn't exist any longer,' Zoe commented.

Once again she had said the wrong thing. A terrible melancholy fell over Le Grand Alain, and he relapsed into silence.

Madeleine appeared, bearing the lamb and flageolet beans on a large, blue dish. 'Smells delicious,' said Judith Fitzwimpleton, her chin shiny beneath her make-up, leaning forward to study the beans.

The Frog, whose head had slumped onto his chest, suddenly came to, revived by the smell of the second course. Picking up his fork, he began poking at the beans like a manic archaeologist.

'I sink we ave a disaster ere,' he announced, as the fork went straight into his mouth. 'I knew it!' he continued, through a mouthful of food. 'These beans are herndercerked! And there hisn't henerf serlt! Ow can Zoe heat flageolet beans hin this cerndition? Do I ave to do heverysing myself?' He pushed back his chair and stormed out of the room with the dinner.

Russell, who had been rearranging the folds of his red and yellow bowtie throughout this contretemps, broke the stunned silence around the table. 'What a tiresome fuss about a few white beans that look like maggots. Sorry, Madeleine, but the French have such strange ideas about food.'

'I eard that!' the Frog shouted from the kitchen. 'You are a criminerl! You dern't deserve your stermach!'

Russell ignored this outburst. 'The only contribution cooking ever made to civilisation in my opinion,' he continued, 'was nouvelle cuisine.'

'Cerdswellerp!' came a bellow. 'Nouvelle cuisine wers for hidiots! The plates got bigger, the food got smerller. Are you mentally retarded?'

'One of the city's top art curators,' said Russell, raising his voice, 'described my work as grounded in existential impulses with crypto-humanist insights into society's deepest fears. The only time I've ever read anything half as profound about cooking, was the food reviewer who said the avocado shrimp cocktail needed to become more poststructuralist if it wanted to escape from its anti-expressivist image.'

'I ave nevaire eard serch sheet!'

Russell banged down his wineglass, splintering the stem. He wasn't use to being heckled at the dinner table. 'Food critics are becoming almost as important as art curators,' he snapped. 'More and more, they speak the same language.'

'I must say that chefs are also getting very fashionable socially,' Judith Fitzwimpleton remarked. 'I really think it's time we found a suitable chef to include in our circle of friends,' she added to her husband.

'You cerd ave me,' said the Frog, poking his head around the door.

'I'm talking about a real chef, someone with position,'

Judith answered coldly. 'We mix in some very exclusive circles. We must be careful.'

The Frog was crestfallen, and vanished from the doorway.

'Getting back to my last exhibition,' Russell carried on, 'I just wanted to add that the curator described my most important painting as the transformation of reverie into an aesthetic continuity, lent new impetus, from a metaphysical standpoint, by—'

'If you ave to terk so merch about your painting,' interrupted the Frog, reappearing with the lamb and flageolet beans, 'per'aps you sherd ave been a writer. Dern't you sink so, Zoe?'

'Art,' Russell said through clenched teeth, 'is a constant and exhaustive ransacking of one's genius.'

'So's cerking,' beamed the Frog, 'although I find that red wine elps. You cerked the lamb too lerng,' he added, turning to Madeleine. 'Nevaire mind. I hadded serm garlic hand parsley hand a leetle drerp erf wine. Do you ave serm Dijon mersterd? Zoe needs Dijon mersterd with er beans.'

'I rarely eat meat as a matter of fact, and then only white meat, except pigs of course,' said Zoe, indignant at the way the Frog kept co-opting her in his power plays.

The Frog did not reply. He was already halfway through his dinner.

'It's funny you like flageolet beans,' Max remarked.

'I thought you only liked eating food with good figures. The aforementioned capsicums, for instance. And brussel sprouts. Sweet potato, on the other hand,' he added in an aside to Zoe, 'offends his sense of aesthetics.'

The Frog shuddered. 'Erl those bermps!' he agreed, shovelling flageolet beans onto his fork. He raised them to his lips while he was still chewing the last mouthful, watching them like a hawk, in case any of them escaped. He ate like a man who knows there is no time to lose, in this life or any other, thought Zoe, a little miffed by the way he had deserted her as he turned his entire attention to his food again.

'What was it like, growing up in France?' she asked, trying to re-engage him in conversation.

No answer.

'The Frog usually never talks when he's eating,' Max explained. 'He doesn't think the two things should be combined. His lecture during the first course, and his remarks when he first tried the flageolet beans, were the result of force of circumstance.'

'In that case, perhaps I should take a book to dinner tomorrow night,' said Zoe.

The Frog looked up. 'Did you hask me sermsing, Zoe?'

'Oh, never mind,' Zoe sighed, as the Frog helped himself to the rest of her beans.

'You'll get indigestion,' Eva warned him. 'The French always get indigestion. Unlike we Germans, the French don't know the word "restraint".'

'It's nert hin the French language,' the Frog agreed, taking another gulp of wine. Concerned for his kidneys, Zoe poured him some water, but she may as well not have bothered. 'Water is a subversive helement,' the Frog rebuked her, waving away the glass.

Judith and Madeleine rose and started removing the second lot of plates—Judith only doing so to keep from smashing one of the wine bottles over Le Grand Alain's head—while Max brought in the salad.

The Frog's neck seemed to elongate, and periscope-style, he peered this way and that. 'No fromage?' he shouted. 'Bert this his a catastrophe!'

'It's not a catastrophe at all. We're having a very rich almond tart for dessert, and we thought that tart on top of cheese would be too much,' Max replied.

'I agree,' said Eva, doing a few, quick upper-arm exercises. 'Why eat until you're going to burst?'

'Why nert?' the Frog demanded. 'Wert is wreng with that? I ham French! I need fromage! There his a procedure that merst be ferllowed!' He threw Max a reproachful look.

'Have some salad,' suggested Zoe. 'It will help fill in the hole.' She was beginning to feel oddly protective of the Frog.

'Hokay,' he said. 'You are the honly wern who cares about me, Zoe.'

She studied him as he ate. 'You're very Kafkaesque, aren't you?' she eventually remarked.

'Ham I?' replied the Frog with interest.

'Mmm. Kafka's preoccupation was the individual's sense of estrangement or alienation in his normal environment.'

'Jerst like me,' the Frog agreed. 'The honly henvironment where I nevaire feel alienated, his hin the kitchen. Shall we ave a serieuse relationship, Zoe?'

'Don't rush her,' advised Antarctica, as Madeleine left the table to fetch the almond tart. 'You have to learn the implications of resituating your emotions during impulsive mood swings.'

'I ham a very himperlsive person!' bellowed the Frog. 'Hit's wern herf my greatest charms!' he added, as Judith Fitzwimpleton stared at him in total disbelief. 'Oh la la la la la la!' he carried on, rocking and wailing like a pilgrim when Madeleine returned with the fourth course.

First he protested that the tart was so gorgeous he could not bear to gaze upon its almond crust. Then, on announcing that he couldn't eat another thing, he accepted a huge helping and, long before the others had finished eating, asked if he could have some more. One portion of the tart remained uneaten.

'I'll ave it,' he volunteered, reaching across the table.

'Donald hasn't had a second helping yet,' snapped Judith.

'Too late!' squealed the Frog, grabbing the tart from off the dish.

'Actually,' said Donald, 'I didn't even manage to finish my first helping. France's representative stole it from my plate while I was having my glass of wine refilled.'

Madeleine sent a warning look to Max, who was trying to control his laughter. 'I'll make you a fruit salad, Donald. There are raspberries and cream in the fridge, and I'm sure Le Grand Alain will help me slice up some bananas.'

'Himperssiberl,' the Frog corrected her. 'I ave to leave himmediately hif you hinsist ern this.'

'Why?' Madeleine asked blankly.

'Bercurse I cannert bear to lerk hat bernernas hany mere. They remind me erf the cernstant herrections I ad when I wers yerng.'

'That does it,' said Donald, pushing back his chair.

'Yes, come and dance!' cried Madeleine, who was sitting next to him. She grabbed his hand. 'I'll put on some Edith Piaf.'

'Nert Piaf,' protested the Frog. 'She's so hover hemotionerl.'

Russell, who had already left the table in order to examine the sculpture of the torso on the stand, turned around. 'This is a really beautiful piece of work, Madeleine. Did you buy it locally?' he asked.

'Le Grand Alain made it,' Madeleine replied, as she and Donald danced stiffly up and down the room. 'It's a plaster mould of my body. Everyone comments on how real the flesh looks. Donald, do you mind not standing on my toes? He really has a great talent. The Frog, I mean. One year he had a sellout exhibition of his body sculptures in the south of France.'

Russell turned abruptly and went outside to join Howard, who was standing at the top of the steps, making notes on his napkin. Zoe, who suspected the notes were about the Frog, commented, 'So you're an artist.'

'Bouf. I ham nert an artist. I like to lerk hat female hanatermy, that's erl. I ate the way heverywern calls himself han artist these days. They erl sink they are Francis Bacern, bert they are nert.'

'Well, if you're not an artist, what are you?' Zoe asked.

'I ham han hexplorer, like Antoine de Saint-Exupéry.'

'Antoine de Saint-Exupéry, aviator, philosopher, and author of *The Little Prince*. I've got his biography at home,' said Zoe. 'Have you ever lived in the Sahara as he did?'

'I drove hover it wernce hin a trerk, which ferll to pieces. I werd like to fly hin a Tiger Merth next time,' the Frog said dreamily. 'Will you haccermpany me, Zoe?'

Zoe was saved the trouble of answering by Russell, who had re-entered the room and obviously wanted to get something off his chest. 'Since you don't claim to have any art credentials, how can you pronounce on who is an artist and who is not?' he barked. 'I doubt you even know the names of any significant paintings. Quick! Don't think! Give me a name—the first one that comes into your head!'

'Goya's *The Burial erf the Sardine*,' beamed the Frog. Oblivious to Russell's outrage, he went on, 'I werd like to merld you, Zoe. Why dern't you cerm hover to my place a few hours earlier termorrow and I will cover you hin plaster befur dinner?'

'I can't,' said Zoe, relieved to have an excuse. 'I have to spend tomorrow looking for another flat. Developers have bought my building in Elizabeth Bay and everyone is being evicted.'

'Houtrageous!' opined the Frog. 'I ate developers! Sydney his becerming a city erf vulgaire leetle rabbit ertches.' He suddenly grabbed Zoe's elbow, spilling some of his wine on the table in his excitement. 'At my flat in Neutral Bay, I ave a wernderfurl spare room with an arbour view,' he told her. 'Why dern't you move hinto my place and write your noverl there?'

Completely taken by surprise, Zoe glanced at Madeleine. 'I'm not sure,' she hedged.

'I think it's a great idea,' Madeleine broke in. 'Ever since you started writing this novel, you've retreated more and more from the real world. The last time I visited you, your flat was full of takeaway sushi trays and your phone had been cut off.'

'Bon! It's settled then!' cried the Frog. 'You ave leeked your lerst sardine can, Zoe! I will cerk—you will write. You will nert heven know I'm there!'

'Somehow I doubt that,' Zoe muttered.

'This means you can cerm with me termerrow, when I go shopping hat the markets,' the Frog went on. 'We will do the berdy merld henerther day. Hat this stage, I sink that sherpping is mere himpertent fur our relationship.'

'We don't have a relationship,' said Zoe, and closed her eyes.

The Frog, ignoring the fact that she seemed to have gone into some kind of trance, leapt to his feet and refilled his glass. 'To celebrate this wernderfurl hevent, I will give a dinner perty!' he cried. 'Heverywern his hinvited. Heven the Pisswomples. Height ho'clock. Dern't be late.'

'You haven't told us when,' Louise pointed out.

'I will announce the date wernce I know wert I ham cerking.'

'I'm not sure that we can make it,' Judith Fitzwimpleton remarked, looking at a point somewhere over the

Frog's shoulder. 'Donald and I are very particular about our food. We eat out several times a week. We like clever, stylish meals, with delicate flavours. What sort of thing do you cook?'

'Rabbit hin red wine! Potatoes hin goose fat! Beef bourgignon, and my famous veal, perk and derk liver terrine, made with brandy, heggs, nertmeg and green peppercerns!' cried the Frog. 'I ave been aving trerble with my cassoulets, bert I sink I ham getting bettaire. My cassoulet his a werk hin prergress—like Zoe's noverl! The honly sing I dern't know ow to cerk,' he added, his face falling slightly, 'his pigs' trertters. Hit's my dream to cerk pigs' trertters. Wern day, I ope sermwern will teach me ow.' He took another large swig from his glass, and his towel, which had been unravelling for some time, fell in a heap on the floor.

Judith screamed and covered her eyes. 'I'm taking you home right now!' cried her horrified husband, helping her from her chair and wrapping his arms around her, shielding her from the sight of the Frog in the raw.

'Bouf!' said the Frog, holding his wineglass in front of him while he unwrapped the tea towel from his neck and bundled it around his nakedness. 'You'd sink she'd nevaire sin a man's privit perts befur!'

'It might be an idea if you went and got dressed,' Madeleine hissed at him.

'Hokay,' the Frog said equably, and strolled out of the room, doing a little wiggle of his buttocks from the doorway. 'Dern't you sink I ave a perky leetle berm, Zoe?' he shouted, before he disappeared from view.

Zoe came to, looking shocked. 'Did I just see the Frog in the flesh from behind?' she gasped. 'I was pondering the enigma of Rimbaud's life. I needed a break from the conversation.'

'Have another glass of wine,' said Madeleine kindly.

By the time the Frog had returned to the dining room, all the guests except Russell and Louise had gone, and Zoe was phoning a taxi. 'Zoe! You're nert going? Where his heverywern?'

'Gone home, or fled home, whichever you prefer,' she replied. 'It's almost two in the morning. I have to get back to my novel. I'm having lunch with Ian, my publisher, in a few days' time and I want the narrative to be perfect by the time I see him. I also have to start packing. What time are you picking me up to go shopping?'

'I will harrive hat two ho'clerk,' the Frog replied. 'This means you can sleep hin, although I like to be han hearly bird, so that I can heat the hearly werm.'

'Crap!' yelled Max, who was opening a bottle of cognac. 'As long as I've known you, you've always stayed in bed as late as possible!'

'That's becurse I ave to recerver frem my sleep!' bellowed the Frog. He held out his glass to Max.

'I think we'll go too,' said Russell, who was still looking disgusted over Le Grand Alain's involuntary striptease. He signalled to Louise. 'When people start shouting at each other, it usually means they've had too much to drink.'

'Herf curse I ave had too merch to drink! Wert's the matter with you?' shrieked the Frog. 'You sink Picasso dranked froshly squizzed horange juice?'

'Max,' said Zoe, breaking into the argument, 'you need to recharge your phone. The red light's flashing. Goodnight. Thanks for dinner.' She pecked him on the cheek and went out into the hall, remarking in a low voice to Madeleine, 'I'm beginning to think that moving in with the Frog is a terrible idea. Why on earth did you talk me into it?'

'You were always the one who wanted to live dangerously,' Madeleine retorted, 'and look at you—locked up day and night with nothing but a laptop for company. The Frog will do you good. Just be careful tomorrow night when you eat the quails.'

'What do you mean?' asked Zoe. 'You think he's going to drug them?'

'No, nothing like that. It's just that—'

Their conversation was interrupted by the taxi driver sounding the horn outside.

The Frog zig-zagged out of the dining room and grabbed Zoe's hand in both of his. 'Zoe! Habout the pigs' trertters! We merst heat them together serm day!'

'Not if I can help it,' answered Zoe.

He stumbled after her into the street. 'I werd take you ome,' he cried, 'bert I cannert furget, I mean remember, where I left my leetle chariot. I sought I perked it—porked it—hin the street houtside the ouse, bert hit's nert there hanymere!'

He reeled back inside, shouting about the mysterious disappearance of his car. 'Bloody foreigners,' said the taxi driver who was Vietnamese Australian. Zoe turned her head as they passed Rushcutters Bay, gazing towards the forest of masts shimmering in the moonlight at the marina. She thought about the solitude that writers craved—the tyranny of routine abandoned and forgotten. No noise. No interruptions. And, above all, no set mealtimes.

When Zoe walked into her flat in a quiet cul-de-sac in Elizabeth Bay, there was a message on her answering machine. Kicking off her shoes and tossing her bag onto her bed, she sank down onto the only other piece of furniture, aside from her desk, that she possessed—a red leather armchair, cracked and worn at the seams.

'Allo,' cried a familiar voice, when she pushed the message button. 'Max made me ave hanerther cognac. I ham nert drernk, certainly nert! Bert when I ferll—folled?—hinto the fig tree hin the garden, Madeleine said I had to sleep ere tonight. Bon nuit, Zoe. I ham going to gave erp smerking jerst fur you. Merde…Why his the red light flashing ern the phern? I ate pherns! I ham nevaire using a phern hagain!'

Zoe was fast asleep on her stomach, dreaming of having sex with Bulgakov. The duvet had slipped onto the floor, and a money-spider, so tiny it might have been a speck of dust, ran down her back and over the slender curve of her hip. Perhaps the spider also dreamed of living in the Sahara.

The phone shrieked into life somewhere close by her pillow. Zoe groaned. Her hair, which was cut in a fashionably tousled style, fell over her face as she sat up. She wondered where she had left the wretched thing. Somewhere on top of a pile of books, no doubt. Or maybe under Vargas Llosa. She checked. It wasn't there.

She staggered around the flat until she found the phone buried in a pile of Alberto Moravia paperbacks on the bench in the kitchen—if a bar-fridge and a microwave in a cupboard could be called a kitchen.

'Whoever you are,' she said, pulling on a sarong with her free hand, 'I hope you know you're interrupting a writer at work.'

'Merde!' screamed the voice at the other end of the line. 'My feets ave grown heven bigger hin the night, and I can't pert ern my shoes.'

'Why are you ringing me at this hour?' Zoe demanded, peering at her watch which she was still wearing. 'It's only nine o'clock.'

'The day is alf finished. We ave to buy the quails.'

'I thought,' said Zoe, trying to remember where the coffee was, 'you were going to let me sleep in. I mean, work.'

'You ave to find a removalist!' the Frog bellowed. 'The sooner you merve hin with me, the bettaire! You nevaire heat. Madeleine terld me. That's why you are so sin.'

'Food is of no consequence when you're a writer. You must starve in order to create.'

'Zoe! This his blosphomy!'

'Stop shouting. I like my mornings to be peaceful,' said Zoe. 'Aren't you ever quiet?'

'Wert is the point herf being quiet, if nowern hever listens to me? When are you cerming?'

'I'll see you at two o'clock,' said Zoe firmly—she had just found the coffee on top of Nabokov—and hung up.

At half past one, her security buzzer sounded.

'I don't believe it,' she muttered, dropping an armful of clothes into the suitcase she had opened.

'Allo Zoe! I ham houtside!'

'I'm not ready!' she shouted at him.

'Zoe, please don't shout. Why cern't people hever cerm when I call? Why do I erlways ave to wait? I am erlways ern time! Why can't hanywern helse be? Wert his their preblerm, hexactly?'

'Okay, okay, I'm coming,' Zoe cried, fed up with the monologue. She put on her black stretch jeans, a black T-shirt, black loafers, the black cap and her dark glasses, and went down into the street. The Frog was leaning against an old green Peugeot, unshaven, in the same pair of jeans he had worn the night before, the same red cotton jumper—sans shirt—and a white silk aviator's scarf tossed around his neck.

'Don't you ever change your clothes?' said Zoe.

'Bouf! I changed my hunderpants—that's good henerf. Do you erlways wear black, Zoe?' he said, looking her up and down.

'Yes. The literary world demands it. Haven't you ever noticed how people who write romantic fiction wear bright colours?' She added, gesturing towards his cigarette. 'I thought you'd given up.'

'I tried, bert my nicotine patch kept ferlling herf. That's why I cannert give herp smerking.'

He took her hand and kissed it. Zoe was getting to quite like this ritual, although she did wish that he had shaved. She got into the car and noticed a large roll of toilet paper sitting on the back seat. Better not to ask, she decided.

'Where did you find the chariot?' she said instead, aware that she was falling into the Frog's peculiar use of language, as if she had known him all her life.

'Houtside a leetle bar, hin the street haround the cerner frerm Max and Madeleine's. The prerblerm wers, I ad erlready gern to the per-leece station, hand reperted the chariot sterlen. I returned and terld the per-leece that sermwern ad made a mernkey hout herf me, and I werd be hobliged if they werd keep an eye hin fur this criminerl hin the future.'

'Keep an eye out,' Zoe corrected him.

'It makes mere sense to keep your eye hin,' the Frog argued. He turned on the engine and they drove off down the street. 'I ham going to sing,' he announced.

'Not "The Marseillaise" again?' Zoe complained.

'Mais non. I shall sing han erld, pernographic French serng. Do nert werry—you will nert hundersternd the werds.'

'Why do you have to sing at all?' Zoe asked.

'So I dern't sink habout the orror ahead,' the Frog explained, and without explaining what this 'horror' might be, clasped a hand on his chest and proceeded to bellow a melody in rich, operatic tones.

'What horror?' Zoe asked, the moment the Frog drew breath. 'Do you mean decapitated quails?'

But her chauffeur didn't reply. They had just left Elizabeth Bay, joining the mainstream Saturday-morning traffic when, without warning, the Frog changed into a man sent crazy by the relationship between twentieth-century mankind and the car.

'Jellyfish!' he screamed, as they were surrounded by a sea of other vehicles, all exercising their democratic right to take up room on the road. 'Lerk hat them! Jellyfish erl hover the place. Wert are they doing ere? Why dern't they stay at ome? Alors, cretin!' he shouted, almost driving into the car next to them. The driver turned his head to see where all the noise was coming from. 'Get hout herf my way, you hidiot! Lerk hat is stupid face! Hin-bred! E lerks like a goat!'

'My God,' said Zoe, tightening her seatbelt. 'You can take the motorist out of Paris, but you can't take Paris out of the motorist.'

'I ham going to take a shert-cert, hin horder to get away frem erl these merons!' raged the Frog.

They forced their way across two lanes of traffic,

swerved around a corner into Paddington, and sped down a civilised, residential street, alive with the sounds of Phillip Glass. A jogger, red-faced, middle-aged, his T-shirt drenched with sweat, came into view. The Frog stuck his head out the window and yelled at the hapless man, 'Why do you berther hat your hage?' Another resident was washing his car. 'Don't forget to mow your lern!'

The only person to win his approval was a brunette in a micro mini-dress, who had opened the boot of her car and was bending over to pick up her sports bag from the pavement. 'Quelle cul!' whistled the Frog, reducing his speed and continuing to ogle her in the rear-vision mirror. 'I ave to wertch herther wormens,' he explained earnestly to Zoe. 'Hertherwise, I werd shriverl herp like a leetle plant withhout werter.'

Zoe had slid right down in her seat, hoping that no one she knew would recognise her. This part of Paddington was full of literary critics and book reviewers, and it was important that she didn't blow her reputation. Image was everything in Sydney. It was all very well writing a book, but you had to be seen to have gravitas, and so did the people you were spotted in public with. The Frog definitely didn't have gravitas. She pictured taking him to drinks at the Sydney Writers' Festival, and blanched.

They swerved around another corner, which brought them back into the thick of the traffic. Zoe saw a light ahead turn red, and braced herself.

'Why his heverywern slowing dern? Wert's wreng with them? Why dern't they speed erp hinstead? People sherd stert a revolution! They sherd blew herp erl the traffic lights—that's wert we do hin Paris!'

'Really?' Zoe commented. 'Why is the congestion even worse there?'

'That's why I came to Sydney!' roared the Frog, managing to miss the point completely. 'Ow did I know the traffic werd ferllow me?'

The lights flashed green, and the cars started moving—although not quickly enough. Just as the Frog reached them, the lights turned red.

This time he went ballistic, banging his fists down on the steering wheel before getting out of the car and pounding his fists on the roof.

'What's the rush?' Zoe asked, bewildered, when he got back in again. 'We've got all afternoon.'

'Nevaire, hevaire, say that to me hagain! Ow do I know ow merch time I ave left to me hin this life?'

By the time they reached Centennial Park, where Sydney's central markets were located, Zoe was a nervous wreck. Her heart began to beat wildly as the Frog let out a long, drawn-out snarl. 'What's the matter now?' she whimpered. Then she saw them. Speed-humps.

'Stery erf my life!' bellowed the Frog. 'Erlways serm-sing to get hin my way! I ham going to drive hover them as fast as I can!'

And he did.

It was after 2.30 p.m., and dozens of motorists were searching for vacant parking spaces. The markets covered at least a third of the space once occupied by the showgrounds. The rest was taken up by Rupert Murdoch's Fox Studios. Beyond the carpark, crowds of people were moving towards avenues of brightly striped canvas awnings, beneath which were displays of fruit and vegetables from all over the South Pacific. The fish, meat, game and cheese were inside a huge building on the left.

A gold Mercedes, driven by a thickset man with gold chains around his neck, edged alongside the Peugeot.

'Visigerth! Vulgaire leetle twerp!'

'God, calm down will you?' Zoe said with embarrassment, winding up her window.

'Why?' the Frog demanded furiously. 'Lerk at wert I ave to pert herp with!'

Zoe glanced again at the Mercedes driver, but he had begun backing into a parking space that had just become available behind them. She then realised that the Frog's abuse was directed at a couple who had got into a car on the left, but were in no hurry to leave. First, the driver, an overweight man with ginger hair, fiddled with the rear-vision mirror and started searching for something on the back seat. His wife, who was wearing a tight, white pair of jeans and bright red sandals with stiletto heels, got out of the car to retrieve a salami that she had dropped on the ground.

'They're doing hit ern perpose!' screeched the Frog.

'For goodness sake!' exclaimed Zoe. 'There's another parking space just ahead. Why don't you take it instead?'

'Oui! I will!' the Frog agreed. 'Furkwerd!' he shouted at the other driver as they passed.

'Fuckwit,' Zoe corrected him, opening the door and getting out, the perspiration damp on her forehead. 'If you have to use such language.'

'I ham learning Hinglish,' the Frog replied grandly, swinging his legs out of the car. He regarded the parking meter with contempt. 'I refurse to pert a coin hin their putred leetle machine. It's jerst hanerther herbstercle hin my way. Perking his a uman right! Let's prerceed directly to the bazaar.'

Whistling the theme from *A Man and a Woman*, he tucked his arm through Zoe's as they walked towards the popular new Sydney markets. They passed a young Pacific Islander sitting surrounded by buckets of sunflowers. Close by, stands were filled to overflowing with pale brown farm eggs, organically grown tomatoes, luscious pink grapefruit, kumara, yams and avocados.

'They ave mere vegetaberls hinside,' explained the Frog, adding, 'I dern't serppose you know that.'

Zoe shook her head. 'I've never been here before.'

'Incroyable! This wers wern herf the first places I came to when I harrived hin Sydney.'

They walked into the main building with its spectacular skylights and original concrete floor, picked up a shopping basket, and threaded their way through the crowd towards the section where chickens, spatchcocks, poussins, quails and ducks were laid out in long rows.

'Don't you lurve the way their leetle lergs sterk herp hin the air?' said the Frog, gazing lovingly at the quails.

'They look so tiny and defenceless,' Zoe answered. 'It's sad to think we kill them just to make a meal.'

'Mais non,' the Frog replied impatiently. 'Quails die hin their sleep.' He selected the plumpest specimens, then led Zoe across the building towards an awe-inspiring display of capsicums. 'Lerk!' he crowed, seizing the most voluptuous capsicum of the lot, and burying his face in its curves. 'Hanerther sexy leetle berm! I merst buy this capsicerm hat wernce!'

'I've never met anyone with a capsicum fetish before,' said Zoe, as he placed it tenderly in his basket.

'Ow merch fur this gergeous leetle sing?' he asked the capsicum-seller, a huge man with a shaven head and a single earring, who looked like he probably did the odd nightshift as a neo-Nazi.

'A dollar ninety-nine,' came the answer.

'You mean two derllars,' the Frog corrected him.

'I mean a dollar ninety-nine.'

'Dern't try to perl the werl hover my heyes with your ridiculous wern derllar, ninety-nine!' shouted the Frog. 'Why dern't you say two derllars hinstead? I ham sick herf this hidiotic ninety-nine cents this, ninety-cents that! Sermsing as to be dern habout it!'

'Here,' said Zoe, handing over the money and dragging the Frog away. 'Do you always have to be so difficult?' she groaned, once they were safely behind some cauliflowers. 'He probably had an iron bar hidden under the sweet potatoes.'

'I'm nert difficerlt,' replied the Frog, astonished. 'Herther people are difficerlt. I ham cerm, huntil sings herpset me. Like now. I sink I ham going to be hill.' He gestured at a pile of kiwifruit. 'I cannert buy hanysing avec fur,' he gulped.

'You peel them before you eat them,' Zoe pointed out.

'I know, bert I ave to lerk hat them first.' He started having some kind of convulsion.

'Quick!' cried Zoe. 'Have the capsicum!'

'Sank you,' said the Frog, burying his face in its curves again. 'You're very kind,' he added, the colour returning to his cheeks.

'Recovered? Good. Let's go and buy the leeks,' said

Zoe briskly. She was beginning to get the hang of shopping with the Frog.

The leek-seller, a more gentle soul, with lank hair and broken veins around his nose, watched as the Frog filled his basket with his produce.

'You eat a lot of leeks,' he commented.

'Bert herf curse,' the Frog replied. 'Leek soup is my religion. It's the ernly stable sing I ave hever known hin my life. When erl is lerst, and erl is lerst a great deal erf the time, I heat soup hin horder to find the strength to carry ern. Soup brings berk memories erf my childhood,' he added, misty-eyed.

'I thought you didn't have any happy childhood memories,' Zoe reminded him.

'No, you are right,' the Frog replied. 'Ow cerd I furget the hevening my trermpert ferll to pieces?'

'I know just how you feel,' said the leek-seller, who was obviously a kind man. 'When I was six, my pit-bull ran into a grain harvester. Never had another dog after that. Tell you what, mate, the leeks are on me.'

'Sank you. You are tres gentil,' the Frog responded, deeply moved. 'I ham very serry about your berll-pert.'

He and Zoe moved off towards the cheese stands, passing, on the way, some people who were handing out pamphlets about a conference soon to be held on the dangers of genetically altered food. 'Bouf! I sink erl erf you need to be genetically haltered first,' the Frog shouted.

'Do you have to comment on everything?' Zoe asked helplessly.

'Herf curse I do!'

She sighed as she watched him toss every variety of cheese he could find on top of the leeks in his basket. 'Do we really need *eleven* chevres and *five* camemberts, apart from all the rest?'

'You can nevaire ave henerf cheese!' pronounced the Frog. 'Dern't be so Hanglo-Saxon, Zoe!'

They then joined the line of shoppers queueing up to pay. Within seconds the Frog was fuming over the time it took to get to the cash register. Zoe thought he'd let fly with a stream of ripe French insults when their turn finally came. But perversely, the Frog paused and turned instead to the woman standing behind them. 'Is that erl you ave?' he said to her. The woman, whose basket contained two items, looked uncertainly at the unshaven Frenchman in the flamboyant, white silk aviator scarf. 'Why dern't you go ahead with your ferny leetle cabbage hand your brie?' he invited her.

Stunned by such thoughtfulness, the woman effusively wished him a very nice day. 'Bouf!' her benefactor replied, his mouth going down at the corners. 'A nice day. His serch a sing perssiberl? Per'aps. I dern't sink so. Bert sank you hanyway.'

'You have to make a speech about everything, don't you?' Zoe said. 'Couldn't you have just thanked her and left things at that?'

'I can nevaire leave sings hat that,' the Frog admonished her. 'I ham French. I ave to make a point.'

As they left the building, he lectured her on the great necessity of argument, which, he was at pains to explain, enjoyed divine status in France. 'Hanglo-Saxons merst learn to hexpress their views,' he pontificated. 'When sermwern says, "ave a nice day," sherd you jerst accept this without sinking? Herf curse nert! Wert appens if there's a ternhado? Merde!' he interrupted himself. 'We furgert the wine! Ow did that appen?'

It was after four o'clock by the time they left the markets. As they made their way back through the rows of parked cars, the Frog reared up, twitching, like a mongoose that has smelled a snake.

'Oh no,' Zoe moaned, as he hurried towards a parking warden who was writing out a ticket in the distance.

'Wert do you sink you're doing?' the Frog was shouting at the official by the time she had caught up with him.

'It's not our car!' Zoe pointed out, praying that the parking warden was a born-again Christian.

'That his nert the point!' yelled the Frog. 'The next sing, this hidiot will stert pertting tickerts hon children riding bicycles sans elmets! You werdn't ave a clue wert a cassoulet is, werd you?' he carried on, turning back to the parking warden. 'And I bet you use a bread and buttaire plate!'

'What's wrong with using a bread and butter plate?' Zoe asked.

'Perking tickerts, seatbolts, cernderms, vaccinations, pesturised cheese, bread and buttaire plates—no wernder Hanglo-Saxons are so cernsterpated!' bawled the Frog. 'We live hin an hover-protected, hover-regulated society perpetuated by merons like you! The French—we perk ern the pavement if we wernt to, becurse we do nert care about the rules. We dern't need bread and buttaire plates becurse we dern't care habout the crembs!'

The parking warden, bug-eyed at this onslaught, tried his best to defend himself. 'You wear red socks, mate,' he said. '*Red socks*. Like a girl.'

'These are my cardinerl serks,' replied the Frog. 'They merst be and-wershed with my special Marseilles serp, then drip-dried hover my bain-marie.' He took one sock off, and waved it in front of the parking warden's face. 'Kiss my serk!' he cried.

'That's enough!' Zoe snapped. 'Leave the poor man alone!' She turned and walked off, outraged by the Frog's behaviour.

'An angel from heaven,' stammered the parking warden, falling on his knees.

'Mais non, she's jerst aving han horser's merde,' the Frog retorted, before hurrying after her. 'Zoe, you were hawferl,' he said, as they drove away. 'There's no serch creature as a "poor" perking werden. They are erl criminerls, who merst be stermped hout like grerbs.'

'Did I tell you I found a removalist?' said Zoe, changing the subject. 'I'll be moving in tomorrow, despite the fact I still have grave misgivings about the whole arrangement.'

'You sherd ave terld me habout this befur!' cried the Frog in consternation. As Zoe began to explain why she was so apprehensive, he interrupted impatiently, 'Wert will we ave fur lernch and fur dinner tomorrow night?'

'I haven't the slightest idea,' Zoe replied. 'Why do we have to decide about tomorrow's meals today?'

'You herndersternd nussing, like erl Hanglo-Saxons!'

'I'll tell you what I don't understand,' said Zoe. 'Why is there a roll of toilet paper on the back seat?'

'Hin case erf hemergencies,' the Frog replied. 'Hanglo-Saxons nevaire sink erf keeping terlet paper hin the car. That's why they're erl cernsterpated.'

'You dislike the English a lot, don't you,' Zoe commented, as they drove across the harbour bridge, past the Opera House and the sun-drenched apartment blocks of Kirribilli.

'I dern't,' the Frog replied, with a surprised glance at

her. 'I like the Hinglish very merch. They know ow to make steak and kidney pie. They live hin castles, and they ave lervely leetle perbs. Best erf erl, I can stretch my legs hout hin their taxis. Bert the Hamericans are hanerther mattaire! They pert pineapperl rings ern heverysing they heat, and they're trying to ruin the French film hinderstry!'

Working himself up into a fresh fury, he drove in typically demented Parisian fashion right across the traffic, wheeled dangerously around some narrow corners, then sped the wrong way up a one-way lane. 'Ere we are hat lerst!' he cried five minutes later, braking without warning. White-knuckled, Zoe stared ahead of her. They had come to a halt right at the edge of the harbour.

After checking her neck for whiplash, Zoe climbed shakily out of the car. The first chance she got she was going to confiscate the Frog's car keys. She stood on the pavement and took a few deep breaths. The street did not literally run into the sea—as she had seen a street do in St Tropez, where she had once spent a summer trying to become the next Marguerite Duras—but it almost did. There was a small grass strip, then some rocks, then the water.

She turned back to the Frog, who was standing on the pavement, staring glumly at the building where he lived. 'Now we ave to climb like mountain goats. I live ern the second fler,' he sighed.

'It looks like a postcard from Tunisia,' said Zoe, determined not to let his negativism get to her. She admired the two-storeyed, whitewashed building with its faded blue front door. The North Shore seemed to specialise in buildings like these—former mansions converted into apartment blocks and now going to seed.

The Frog led the way along the pavement and up some old stone steps. A colony of lizards, sunbaking in the cracks like tiny, dark green jewels, scattered in all directions as they approached.

Zoe watched, amazed, as he went purple in the face trying to get his key into the door of his apartment. 'I ate lerks! Hever since I wers bern, lerks ave tried to erbstrect my life! You ave to pert a key hinto a door to make hit hopen—it cannert hopen by itself. Herf curse nert! That werd be too heasy, werdn't hit? Heverysing as to be made cermplicated, jerst so you know you ave no ope! I ham cursed hin this life. Cursed!'

He got the door open. Zoe followed him through a tiny vestibule into a living space made light and airy by tall windows with ledges wide enough to sit on. Her eyes were drawn to an old refectory table, long enough to throw the kind of decadent dinner party she had always dreamed of having—if only she could cook. The table was covered with debris from meals past, mainly breadcrumbs, wine corks, olive stones and some mouldy Roquefort cheese which appeared welded to the wood.

At the far end of the table an empty gherkin jar sat on top of a teetering pile of books.

'Eh voila!' cried the Frog, opening creaking doors onto a balcony that stretched the length of the apartment, and which was draped at one end in bougainvillea. The light from the harbour shimmered on the walls and on a beautiful piece of furniture standing in the corner on the grubby parquetry floor. 'My grandmerther's secretaire,' said the Frog, his voice softening. 'And that's me, sitting ern my perty.'

Puzzled, Zoe could only see an ancient painting of Venice in a rather battered gilt frame, leaning against the wall on the secretaire's marble top. Moving closer, she spotted a small black-and-white framed photo of a toddler sitting on a potty, who stared back at her with world-weary eyes. 'What an extraordinary photograph!' she exclaimed. 'I've never seen such a cantankerous-looking child. Were you constipated or something?' This was low, but she felt she had to even the score after all the Frog's insults about Anglo-Saxon bowels.

'Mais non,' he scoffed. 'French childrens are nevaire cernsterpated. We ave goose fat and gherkins mashed hinto our baby food. I wers erlways very herpset whenever I wers furced to sit ern my perty, becerse it wers jerst hernether way erf making me waste my time.'

The wall opposite the secretaire was floor-to-ceiling books. Books stacked in unruly piles, books leaning upside down in a sloppy fashion against each other, books whose spines were in urgent need of repair, books about to topple from great heights. Zoe walked across the room to rescue one that was in imminent danger of crashing to the floor. It was a copy of Henri de Berranger's *Le Vieux Nantes,* and inside, there was the name Denise. 'My grandmerther,' said the Frog, looking over her shoulder. 'Er family came frerm Nantes. Shall we ave a glass erf wine?'

'Why don't you let it breathe?' Zoe suggested, replacing the book.

'Bouf! It can breathe while we drink hit!' the Frog replied, taking a bottle of wine from one of the shopping bags.

Zoe walked out on the balcony from where there was a perfect view of ferries criss-crossing the harbour. 'All this place needs,' she mused, studying the bougainvillea spilling down into the overgrown garden, 'is the eyes of a tiger peering from the greenery, like one of Rousseau's paintings.'

It really was like a jungle, with thick clumps of banana-palms and mature Chinese money trees. In one corner some long-stemmed crimson flowers had forced their way through the other plants, and a spectacular tree fern had grown to the same level as the balcony railing. A scarecrow, dressed in shorts, a mulberry-coloured shirt and a beret, was stretched out in a deckchair in its shade.

'Did you make that scarecrow?' Zoe asked the Frog, as he joined her at the balcony's edge.

'Oui. E reminds me erf the wern my grandmerther ad hin France.'

'You're quite sentimental, aren't you, despite all your gloom and doom?'

'I ham sentimental fur the France I knew when I wers growing erp,' the Frog replied. 'Life ad a grandeur then, and a lervely mellow querlity. Hevery day wers spent dreaming erf sermmer olidays. Heven the melancholy when the olidays hended, ad a kind erf henchantment.' He looked sad for a moment, and very, very Gallic.

'Why don't you grow some vegetables between the flowers?' said Zoe, knowing that she had to get him back on the subject of food again, fast.

'Nevaire!' roared the Frog, snapping back to life. 'Hit's like the separation between church and state! The two sings merst nevaire be mixed! I cannert find the cerkscrew,' he added crossly. 'Why ders heverysing erlways disappear round ere?'

'Perhaps if you tidied up more,' Zoe answered, following him back inside.

There was no denying the apartment's appeal, but its charm had been ruined by ashtrays overflowing with olive stones, shoes everywhere, dirty wineglasses and, in every direction she looked, empty gherkin jars.

Above a dark green armchair hung a portrait of

Bonaparte and, next to it, a Brassai photograph of some elderly men drinking wine in a cafe. Their expressions were so doleful that Zoe felt depressed as well.

'Oui, that's me hin hernerther few years,' remarked the Frog, as he took the quails into the kitchen.

Zoe flinched when she saw the profusion of unwashed saucepans, sheets covered in flecks of plaster on the floor, and what looked like a lobster claw poking up from the sink. 'Is it always this messy?' she asked, more rudely than she had intended, stepping over yet another empty gherkin jar to examine a half-finished sculpture of the outstretched fingers of a hand that was covering a voluptuous female breast.

'I did nert realise you were serch a bourgeois, Zoe,' said the Frog, watching her with a frown. 'The kitchen his where I hexpress myself. Cerking, merlding, making lerve hermerngst the petit pois—wert's wreng now?' She had come to a halt in front of a small, grotesquely grinning doll positioned on the windowsill, with a vegetable knife pushed right through its stomach.

'You're not into voodoo, are you?' said Zoe, shaken by the sight. 'If that's the case, I won't be moving in, you know.'

'Sermtimes,' said the Frog grimly, 'drostic measures merst be taken!'

'But who's it meant to be?'

'Z,' he snarled, naming a famous cookery writer

whose book *Cooking—It's a Piece of Cake* had just reached number one on the bestseller lists. 'She his a criminerl who has hinserlted a great hart, and she merst serffur the consequences. Don't werry about er, Zoe—she's getting wert she deserves! The prerblerm is, I'm going to need that vegetaberl knife to cherp my leeks.' He turned and gestured at rows of vegetable peelers hanging on the wall. 'Wert do you sink erf my cerllection?' he asked. 'They come frerm erl hover the world.'

'I've never met anyone who collects vegetable peelers,' Zoe commented, making a mental note to ring Howard as soon as possible. She gestured at an empty hook at the end of the row. 'What happened to that one?' she asked.

The Frog glowered. 'A terrible tragedy!' he shouted. 'I cannert bear to sink habout hit! Soon after I harrived hin Sydney, I ad a leetle flung.'

'You mean a "fling",' Zoe translated.

'Wern night I cerked er my special potatoes hin goose fat,' the Frog went on. 'Hafterwerds, I discerverd she ad thrown the vegetaberl peeler hout avec the peelings! That's wert appens when you let houtsiders hinto your kitchen! I spent erl night searching fur my leetle peeler, bert I nevaire saw hit hagain!'

'Why don't you show me my room?' suggested Zoe, impatient to see her new writing and sleeping quarters.

'Bouf! Why do you need your hown room?' scoffed

the Frog. 'My bed his big henerf fur two. Hokay, hokay—why nert, fur the furst few days?' Muttering about what a ridiculous waste of time it all was, when soon they would be lying in each other's arms in ecstasy, he led Zoe down the little hall towards the vestibule.

'What, you mean the broom cupboard?' she said in disbelief, as the Frog waved her towards the door behind the hat-stand.

'Why dern't you lerk hinside befur you fly hunder the andle?' the Frog retorted, standing aside and gesturing at her to go ahead of him. Zoe pushed past him, then stopped, amazed, on the threshold. Not only was the room huge, there was an ocean liner heading straight towards her. 'It's a wernderfurl herpticerl hillusion, no?' enthused the Frog. 'I werd sleep hin ere myself, bert I like to be closer to the kitchen.'

Zoe was entranced. The room had been painted white, and its windows opened right into the harbour—at least that's the impression she got as the ocean liner slowly turned and filled the entire view. It was exactly the kind of room she had imagined herself living and writing in, with all due respect to Proust, of course. Cork-lined rooms weren't quite her style. And besides, this would be a far better room to be photographed in, when her book was finally published. It had great dramatic potential, and would add to her image immensely. She thought of the chapter in Claudio Magris's book *Danube*, about Hoffman's Baron von R, 'who travelled the world collecting views, and whenever he thought it necessary in order to enjoy or create a fine panorama, had trees cut down, branches stripped, humped surfaces smoothed, entire forests flattened and farms demolished…When a wall of foliage suddenly fell, opening out a vista towards a distant castle in the light of sunset, Baron von R remained for a few minutes gazing upon the spectacle that he himself had staged, and then hurried away, never to return.'

'Baron von R could not have bettered this view,' she commented, reluctantly turning away from the window to inspect the rest of the room. 'My exercise bike can go at the end of my bed,' she went on. 'I ordered it over the phone this morning from the sports store Eva recommended, and the removalists are going to pick it up for me.'

'Do you really sink you will use your hexercise bike?' the Frog inquired.

'Every day,' said Zoe. 'I don't want to be flabby. Imagine a flabby writer on the cover of *Vanity Fair*.'

'So you like the hapartment?'

'It's not exactly the villa next door to Gore Vidal's in Ravello, but it will do,' Zoe allowed. Privately, she was thrilled, and looked forward to sitting on the balcony watching the harbour in all its moods—as well as the 'diffused white light of overcast skies, and the dark grey light of storms', as Marguerite Duras once wrote about Trouville.

'Bon! I'll go and stert preparing the soup,' said the Frog, breaking into her thoughts.

'I'll come with you,' Zoe answered, suspecting her role was to stand by and admire him. Never mind. It would be a way of repaying him for the room—apart from paying rent, she meant.

But the Frog waved her away as she followed him into the living room. 'I do nert wernt you hin my kitchen. You will honly hinterfere. I sought I made this clear? You merst nevaire, hevaire, henter my domain without hasking.'

'You're not serious?' said Zoe. 'I'm going to be living here as well, you know.'

'That his nert the point! I terld you befur—I will cerk, you will write! Hanyway, I dern't wernt you lerking hin my secret cerpberds.'

'Let me make sure I've got this right,' said Zoe. 'You don't want me in the kitchen under any circumstances.'

'Cerrect.'

'And you intend to do all the cooking.'

'Oui.'

'And you'll also do the cleaning up?'

'Bouf! Wert cleaning herp? It ernly takes five minutes.'

Zoe was silent. It sounded too good to be true. Or was this cooking routine just another sordid French ruse to get her into bed? Of course, she thought, that had to be it. You would think that sharing a flat with a writer would be exciting enough without wanting sex as well. She suspected, however, that once the Frog realised she wasn't going to acquiesce, he'd expect her to start cooking some if not all the meals. And that was going to be a problem because she didn't have a culinary clue. 'Although I do a very nice salad,' Zoe said aloud, clutching at straws.

'Wert did you say?'

'It doesn't matter.'

'Why dern't you hinvestigate the rest erf the hapertment?' suggested the Frog, disappearing into the kitchen.

Zoe stood there, pondering her predicament. There was only so much takeaway sushi she could eat in her lifetime, and the Frog's revelation about Camus had really shaken her. She should have been firmer about spelling out the situation regarding their relationship, but it was too late for the moment. She'd enjoy her free meal tonight and see what happened after that.

Fifteen minutes later Zoe walked into the kitchen gingerly holding an empty box of herrings and a discarded toothpaste tube covered in green mould, which she dropped into the garbage.

The Frog, busily chopping up onions and leeks, frowned at her incursion. 'Since this his your first time ere, I'll make han hexception. Bert make sure you dern't get hin my way,' he said, handing her a glass of wine.

'Why is there a box of herrings in the bathroom?' Zoe asked.

'Hin case I get lerked hin. I do nert wernt to sterve to death,' the Frog replied.

'But the box was empty.'

'So wert? I got angry when I wers shaving.'

'And the brioche on your bedside table?'

'Hin case I get angry hin the night. You might get angry hin the night too,' the Frog added hopefully.

Zoe flushed. She hadn't meant to admit she'd looked around his bedroom. She just wanted to check out whether it was true that a Frenchman's bed mirrored his sexual technique. A friend who had slept with several French men claimed they sprinkled their pillows with Chanel No 5 to urge the shyer women on, and trailed silken cords suggestively over the bedhead, in memory of *The Story of O*. The moment she walked into the Frog's bedroom she knew her friend had lied. His unmade bed had a medical dictionary sticking out from under one very squashed pillow, and there was an empty jar of gherkins lying next to it. A computer, a banana chair listing to stern beneath a pile of clothes, and an ancient and very battered steamship trunk, which had a sticker, 'Cairo Canapes' prominently displayed on one side, were the sole furnishings. A single, silver candlestick on the bedside table might have been nice—but no. That had been reserved for the brioche. And then there was his bed linen.

'How many grown men,' she asked him in the kitchen, 'sleep in sheets decorated with little blue and red boats?'

'I like my sheets,' the Frog said sulkily. 'When I go to sleep, I dream I'm aving hadventures ern the Hamazon. My grandfurther ad lerts herf hadventures wern e wers yerng. The steamship trunk belernged to im. E wers a great hexplorer. E went to Vietnam and smoked lerts erf hopium.'

'And the sheets are filthy. When were they last washed?' Zoe went on, refusing to be distracted by his family history.

'I sought writers liked dirty sheets,' replied the Frog defensively.

She snorted. 'You've been reading too much Henry Miller.'

'Merde!' the Frog suddenly bellowed. 'I forgot to rerll erp my sleeves, and now I've got buttaire erl hover them! I sherd nevaire wear clothes hin the kitchen! I sherd cerk completely knackered!'

Zoe, recalling the quick glimpse she got of the Frog's buttocks rotating in the doorway of Max and Madeleine's dining room, said quickly, 'Why don't you wear short sleeves to cook?'

'I nevaire wear short sleeves! Short sleeves are fur peasants! They sherd ernly be wern hin han hemergency—hif your car sinks hin the river, fur hexamperl!'

'But why would the car sink in a river?'

'That his nert the point! Do you erlways take heverysing so literally, Zoe?'

'What are these secret cupboards you mentioned earlier?'

'That's where I keep my hemergency serpplies. Dern't you hever dare try to lerk hinside!'

'I think I'll go outside and leave you to your paranoia,' snapped Zoe. She caught sight of the cupboard he was talking about. It was padlocked.

If only the Frog would stop being so volatile the entire time, she thought, as she leaned against the balcony railing, watching a yacht heading towards Circular Quay, she might get to like him. His taste in literature wasn't bad, and he had a full set of Georges Simenon's Maigret novels, in English, on his bookshelves. She had always wanted to read them. But as for anything more deep and meaningful—it simply wasn't on the cards. 'You see,' she explained to the Frog, when he came out triumphantly brandishing the corkscrew, 'I always imagined I'd be a woman written to—you know, like Milena Jesenska and Kafka. If you and I had an affair, I'd have to accept a collection of vegetable peelers as the equivalent of a passionate literary correspondence, and how would that look in later years when my life and work is written about in the *New York Review of Books*?'

'Werd you like to cerm and watch me sterff the quails?' replied the Frog.

'Oh, why not,' said Zoe, giving up.

The birds were laid out on the kitchen table, for all the world like bodies waiting to be identified. 'Lerk at my leetle treasures!' cried the Frog, pressing the stuffing he had made into their plump little bellies with gusto.

To her deep dismay, Zoe felt hunger pangs. 'I feel like a traitor,' she remarked, as the Frog put the birds into the oven. 'You just don't get the same feeling with sushi.'

'Nert heating his the betrotal.'

'You mean, betrayal.'

'Bouf! Wertever! Let's ave a glass herf wine.'

The moon appeared over the treetops of Kirribilli, creating a silver path across the bay. Zoe realised that she hadn't thought once about Bulgakov, from the moment she took her first mouthful of leek soup. She had never tasted soup like it. She could feel it unlocking her literary imagination. 'Camus, here I come,' she said.

'Nowern cerks leek soup like me,' the Frog nodded, adjusting the tea towel around his neck. 'Bert my quails taste heven bettaire. Why dern't we heat them hin my bedroom? It's mere cermfertaberl hin there. You know,' he confided, 'sermtimes when I ham erl halone, I take a quail leg to bed.'

'No wonder your sheets are so grubby,' Zoe commented.

Crestfallen, the Frog departed to fetch the second course, re-emerging in a happier mood with the roasted quails sizzling away in an oven dish. 'Lerk at their bloated stermachs,' he gloated. 'That his real sterffing, Zoe! Hanglo-Saxons ave no idea. They sink hit's erl dern with breadcrembs.'

The quail, served with petit pois, were so delicious that she devoured three of them without stopping. Remembering Madeleine's anxiety, she chuckled. What dreadful scenario had her best friend been imagining? 'May their souls rest in peace,' she said, placing her knife and fork over the little carcasses. She looked across at the Frog with a smile. 'Is something wrong?' Zoe asked with a sinking heart.

He had turned an awful, mottled red colour, and was spluttering incoherently. 'Wert is that...*hatrocity*?' He was barely able to get the words out. He gestured at the remains of the quails on her plate. 'It's diabolicerl!'

'What are you talking about?' said Zoe in bewilderment, looking down at her plate, then back up at him.

'You ave *massacred* my quails! I ave nevaire seen serch a carnage hin my life!' He got up from the table in a fury, ripping off his tea towel and flinging it on the floor as he left the room.

Zoe sat there. What was quail meant to look like after being eaten? Was that what Madeleine had been trying to warn her about? She studied her plate carefully, then the Frog's.

Things became clearer. The Frog's quail bones lay in a simple, yet intricate pattern, whose perfection suggested the culinary version of haiku. Each bone was balanced perfectly on the one below, in an arrangement somehow suggesting both the obscurity and nobility of existence.

Her bones looked like the culinary version of a car-wrecking yard, or a funeral pyre which a herd of elephants had stampeded through. Well, he'd simply had more practice than she had, that was all. Wiping her hands on her napkin, Zoe went off to find her hysterical host.

She found him sitting in front of the computer in his bedroom. 'What are you doing?' Zoe asked him cautiously.

'I'm hemailing Max,' barked the Frog, without

turning around. 'E sherd ave reminded me that Hanglo-Saxons ave no idea ow to heat hanysing with burns. I know hit's nert your furlt, Zoe—you cannert elp your hancestry. Bert hernestly! You merst nevaire do that to me hagain!' His shoulders sagged as he spoke, and Zoe felt a twinge of remorse.

'Have you ever read any haiku?' she asked in a conciliatory tone. Sitting down on the bed, she quoted, 'Down from the teahouse balcony we cast long fishing lines: the summer moon sailed past.'

Silence.

'Ow did they cerk the feesh?' he asked.

'I don't think I can live here after all,' said Zoe coldly. 'All you think about is food. For you, life is defined by quail leftovers. But for me, it's about ephemeral fictional detours, valid literary devices and the challenge of trying to write in an intellectually legitimate manner that won't confuse my readers—or myself. So, in the circumstances, I think I'm going to have to find somewhere else to live.'

The Frog deleted the message to Max and leapt to his feet, kicking over his glass of wine. 'Zoe! You cannert keep writing ern han hempty stermech. Your noverl wern't be perblished fur years! Horsers are getting yernger erl the time. You merst reconsider.'

'I'll think about it,' Zoe replied. The Frog's words had struck a nerve.

'I wers going to cerk my special feesh soup with garlic crouterns tomorrow night—and creme caramel fur dessert,' the Frog continued. 'Sherd I berther to cerk fur you, er nert?'

'I'll call you with my decision when I get home.'

'You're going ome now?' said her host, looking most put out. 'Bert we aven't ad the fromage! I cannert believe this his appening hagain! Two fromage-free hevenings hin a row!'

'I'm sure you can eat the cheese on your own,' said Zoe. 'I'm going to call a taxi. No,' she added, holding up a hand, as the Frog grabbed his car keys, 'I don't want a lift. Think about the jellyfish. They'll be out in force. Anyway, *if* I decide to move in tomorrow, I'll need an early night. The removalists are coming at half past nine, and I still haven't finished packing.'

The Frog looked utterly downcast when Zoe left but, by the time she got back to Elizabeth Bay, the answering machine was in an uproar. She grabbed the phone at the third 'Allo!'—cutting him off mid-shout. 'What is it?' she said coolly.

'Wert time will you be ere termorrow merning?'

'Sometime after eleven, I suppose,' Zoe replied, completely forgetting that she had intended to keep the Frog on ice a little longer.

'Bon! Fur lernch, I sink I'll make a Spernish homolette,' said the voice at the other end of the line. 'I sink that werd be safest.'

'What do you mean?' Zoe asked.

'There are no burns hin Spernish homolettes,' said the Frog, and hung up.

'**E**rry erp!' the Frog shouted at Zoe from the top of the steps outside the building. 'It's erlmost noon! You're late!'

He was wearing white shorts, a red-striped shirt, his boat shoes and the inevitable tea towel over his shoulder. In his hands he held a mixing bowl, which he was peering into as if it contained the secrets of the universe. 'I need you to hundress!' he bellowed. 'I dern't wernt to ave to wait!'

One of the removalists, a big man full of muscles, smirked as he lifted Zoe's desk out of the van. 'Your boyfriend's in a bit of a hurry, isn't he?'

'He's not my boyfriend,' said Zoe, feeling the sun

burning the back of her neck as she stood on the footpath. 'And please be careful with that desk. I'm writing a very important novel on it.'

'I'm a bit of a writer myself,' said the removalist. 'Poetry, mainly.'

'How nice,' said Zoe. 'The bed, the desk and the chair are going in the one room. I'll show you when you get upstairs.' Carrying her overnight bag and her laptop, she walked up the steps to her new home.

'I've decided to merld you befur lernch,' announced the Frog, as Zoe reached him. 'Frem your shurlders to your berm. Do you sink hit has too merch hoil?'

'My bum?' asked Zoe, startled, wiping her forehead. It was hotter than usual for March, and she wished she had worn shorts instead of her black bicycle pants. She had bought the pants last season, but failed to buy the bike.

'Mais non, my mayhonnaise,' the Frog replied, holding out the bowl.

'Looks good,' said Zoe, peering over her dark glasses. She stuck her little finger into the mixture, and then licked it. 'Not bad at all.'

'Bon! We will ave it with serm hasparagers befur lernch.'

'I don't want a big lunch, and I don't want to be moulded today,' Zoe told him, as they walked into the building. 'It's too hot, I've got to unpack, and I'm not sure you should see me naked.'

'Bouf! You sink I ave nevaire sin a naked worman befur,' chuckled the Frog. 'You are so furny, Zoe. Hokay. I'll wait. Bert I hinsist you heat lernch. My Spanish homelette his deevine.'

He explained that he had spent the morning working on the menu for the week. 'Husually, I dern't tell people wert I plan to cerk,' he added. 'And hin future, I will ernly tell you ern a needs-to-know basis wert we're heating. Bert tonight, I can tell you, I ham definitely cerking feesh soup with garlic crouterns, jerst has I premised!'

'Well, I can see why you're moving in,' remarked the other removalist to Zoe, flicking his ponytail off his shoulder as he followed them up the stairs with her new exercise cycle propped on his shoulder. 'Where do you want all those boxes of books in the truck?'

'In the living room,' Zoe answered. She turned to the Frog. 'There's quite a few. You'll have to make some room for them.'

'I horganised my library so that I know *hexactly* where hevery berk his,' the Frog replied with a frown. They walked through the vestibule and across the hall into the living room, where he gazed with pride at the chaos of his bookshelves. 'I like heverysing to be hin horder. I dern't wernt your berks mixed erp with mine.'

'Just show me where the maginot line is,' said Zoe. 'I'm sure we can find room. I need to unpack my books as soon as possible. As a writer, I feel insecure until I see my books around me. It's to do with needing the energy from other writers' words.'

She began pushing the Frog's books closer together, removing some from one shelf altogether and adding them to the piles brushing the ceiling. The removalists returned with the first lot of boxes, and stacked them in a pile in the corner of the room.

'Bouf!' said the Frog, carrying the top box to the table, and rifling through the Russian contingent on top—Chekhov, Bulgakov, Nabokov, Yevgeny Yevtushenko and Anna Akhmatova. 'They sink they know more than Montaigne?'

'Actually, Tolstoy always found the French a bit odd,' Zoe commented, plucking out the author from the second box, where she had mistakenly placed him.

Ignoring this, the Frog continued his inspection. 'Not bad for a Siberian,' he pronounced of Andrei Makine's *Le Testament Francais*. '*And* he lives hin Paris.'

Bertrand Russell got a desultory glance and an unintelligible mutter. 'Bertrand Russell,' said Zoe pointedly, 'once remarked that the desire for food has been, and still is, one of the main causes of great political events.'

'E's got sermsing there,' the Frog conceded, putting Russell on one of his own shelves, and picking up Marguerite Duras. 'Hanerther translation!' he said dismissively, sitting down on Martha Gellhorn, his elbow just missing Helen Garner, Nicholas Jose, Simon Leys and Octavio Paz, and managing to dislodge Bao Ninh, Ryszard Kapuscinski, Frank Moorhouse, David Malouf and Patrick White. 'Wert a lert erf horsers you Hanglo-Saxons ave,' he said, totally disregarding their respective nationalities.

'Your Maigret books are in English,' retorted Zoe, in answer to his first remark.

'I keep them to hentertain stray Hanglo-Saxons,' shrugged the Frog. 'Now, this berk isn't bad fur a fureigner,' he allowed a moment later, waving around a copy of Lowry's *Under the Volcano*. 'This his the stery herf han Hinglish consul, drinking himself to death hin Mexico,' he announced.

'Thanks. I have read it,' said Zoe.

'The Hinglish consul his a great ero hin the French tradition,' the Frog pontificated, as if she hadn't spoken. 'I will pert im next to Proust.' He threw a silky glance her way.

'I have my own copy of Proust, thanks,' said Zoe.

'Hanerther translation,' nitpicked the Frog. Continuing his appraisal of Zoe's reading matter, he flicked his fingers at Norman Lewis—remarking that Malraux had already written all there was to know about Indochina—before inquiring, 'Who's this Timothy Garton Hash?'

'Timothy Garton Ash,' Zoe corrected him.

'Werthever. I dern't know him. *Heat thee Reech* by P. J. Ho Rork. Wert a furny title. His hit a cerkberk?'

'No,' said Zoe shortly.

'And wert habout this wern? *Heat Me* by Linda Jaivin. Wert a nerty horser she merst be!'

'I think we'd better sort something out right now,' said Zoe. 'If we're going to be in constant competition over which of us has the better authors, or if you're going to spend your entire time sniggering at Anglo-Saxon titles, my living here isn't going to work. And stop concealing V. S. Naipaul behind Voltaire.'

'What's this about?' asked the poet-removalist, selecting Peter Robb's *Midnight in Sicily* from more boxes he had just brought in.

'Why don't you lend it to him, Zoe?' the Frog suggested.

'No!' Zoe shrieked. The two men stared at her in amazement, as she snatched Robb from the removalist and stood there, trembling.

'If we're going to share this apartment,' she said, trying to control her voice, 'there's something you're going to have to understand. *I NEVER LEND MY BOOKS!*'

'Why nert?' asked the Frog.

'Because I never get them back! Do you know what it's like to be a writer and to know that some of your most cherished books have gone missing? All of a sudden, you've lost your context! You may as well begin watching commercial television! Why can't people buy their own books, like I do? Cheapskates! *Borrowers*!' She collapsed onto the Frog's sofa and began to sob.

'She asn't heaten today,' the Frog explained to the removalist sotto voce. 'I'll get serm food hinto er, then she'll be hokay.'

'Right,' said the removalist. He made as if to go, but stayed, hovering, by the boxes. Plucking up courage, he asked, 'You haven't got any Sylvia Plath, have you?'

'Get out!' Zoe screamed. She sagged suddenly, and fell back on the sofa in a half faint.

As the removalist fled, the Frog sat down next to her and started spooning mayonnaise into her mouth. 'You're too possessive, Zoe,' he chided her, once she had recovered. 'You ave to learn to share.'

'Like you do in Chinese restaurants?' retorted Zoe, not prepared to sanction the Frog's holier-than-thou act, even though his mayonnaise revived her. 'Madeleine told me. She said you sit at yum cha brandishing your chopsticks and trying to keep all the dishes to yourself.'

'Why sherd I be democratic hin a Chinese restaurant?' the Frog demanded.

'Almost done,' said the ponytailed-removalist five minutes later, poking his head around the door. The Frog went over to the bookshelves, opened Flaubert's *Trois Contes,* and shook out some hundred dollar bills.

'Ere you are,' he said, handing the money to the man. 'I ave to go and stert making lernch.'

'What do you think you're doing?' demanded Zoe. 'I'm paying for the move.' She jumped up and wrote out a cheque. The Frog shrugged and disappeared into the kitchen. 'Thanks,' said the removalist, handing back the Frog's money and edging out the door. 'Good luck with the book.'

Zoe went out onto the balcony, and gulped in great breaths of air. It was difficult having a writer's temperament. Her nerves were so finely strung she could sometimes feel them quiver when she wrote something really good. She went to see what the Frog was doing in the kitchen, forgetting that she wasn't allowed to enter his sacred realm. He was making more mayonnaise. 'Do you always keep cash in your books?' she asked him.

'Oui. And hin my serks. Go haway, Zoe. You are breaking the rules.'

'No bank account?'

'Wert his the point erf aving a bonk haccernt? Bonks steal erl your merney hanyway.'

'You'd better not say that to Max.'

'Max agrees with me. Wern day,' added the Frog, 'I'm going to bury my merney hin a ole hin the garden.'

'Anyone would think you were a peasant,' Zoe remarked.

'I ham a peasant hin my art!' roared the Frog, with a flourish of the mayonnaise whisk. 'Peasants are the soul herf France! Nowern can tell them wert to do! They do hexactly has they please, and tell the pearliticans to get sterffed! Civil disobedience his hin their genes! Zat's why I lerve them very merch! Erl my life, I wernted to be a peasant! '

'You're almost there,' said Zoe, thinking of the toilet paper in the car.

At that moment the most eccentric cat she had ever seen sailed in through the window and landed on the floor with a triumphant little grunt. Its long white fur was matted with twigs and leaves, and its eyes, stern beyond belief, seemed to gaze from an ancient place in some other world.

'This is the Hayatollah, and that wers is Holympic leap,' said the Frog, introducing the creature proudly. 'E lives next door, bert e cerms ere fur erl is meals.' The Ayatollah stared at Zoe, looked inquiringly at the Frog, licked up some mayonnaise which had fallen onto the floor, and vanished back outside.

'Lerk!' cried the Frog. 'E's sitting hin hits leetle perch!' Zoe turned towards the window. The creature was sitting in the middle of the tree fern. 'Wert a clever chat!' The Frog beamed as the cat began to box the fronds. 'E's very sportif, non?'

Zoe, losing interest in the animal, realised to her great relief that the voodoo doll was gone. The Frog, it seemed, had made a big effort to clean up. The dishes had been done, the lobster claw removed and the corkscrew was hanging on the empty hook belonging to the missing vegetable peeler. And the plaster-mould hand on the breast, noticed the previous day, had now been placed in the centre of the table. 'Whose breast is that?' Zoe asked, deciding not to comment on how pronounced the nipple was.

'Ziggi's,' the Frog replied. 'She his very sexy. Er fingers are superb.'

'I didn't realise it was her fingers you were featuring.'

'Ziggi his a concert pianist,' replied the Frog, looking confused. 'That's why she wernted a merld erf er and.'

'Oh, I see. The breast just got in the way.'

'Non, it wers jerst there, so I merlded hit as well. You're nert meant to be hin the kitchen, Zoe,' he reminded her, handing her a glass of wine.

'I don't normally drink at lunchtimes,' Zoe answered, 'but I will today.'

'To celebrate your moving hin with me?'

'When are we eating?' asked Zoe, side-stepping his question.

'Right now! We can heat the asparagers hin the

kitchen, while I cerk the homolettes. The cat will ave lernch with ers has well.'

Zoe and the Frog took their plates through to the table in the living room and glanced out the window. The Ayatollah had gone. 'Nevaire mind. It will be berk later ern. You can ave its homolette if you like,' said the Frog to Zoe.

'I can't believe you made a miniature Spanish omelette for the cat,' she answered. 'But since you did, why don't you give it to him for dinner?'

'The Hayatollah cannert heat a cerld homolette!' cried the Frog. 'E likes is food ot, like me. No, the chat will ave wert we're heating. Hit hadores feesh soup.'

Zoe leaned back in her chair and fanned herself with her napkin. 'It shouldn't be so hot this time of year!' she exclaimed. The Frog poured her another glass of wine. 'It will cool you down,' he said.

'Wine doesn't cool you down,' scoffed Zoe, but she sipped it anyway. A wave of fatigue swept over her, and she yawned.

'I like your bicycle pants, Zoe,' remarked the Frog. 'Ow erften do you sink you'll hactually ride your hexercise bike?'

'I'm going to ride it right now,' said Zoe, refusing to take the bait. 'Then I'm going to have a shower, and then I'll do some work.'

'Ow his the noverl going?'

'It's at an extremely interesting stage.'
'Wert stage his that?'
'It's hard to explain.'
'You sherd ave a cream,' said the Frog.
'A what?'
'A cream. You sherd make sermwern commit a cream. Cream fiction his very populaire.'
'It's not that sort of book,' said Zoe.
'Bouf! You cerd still ave a cream, jerst to livern erp the plert.'
'There is no plot,' Zoe reminded him. 'Plots are for writers of romantic fiction.'
The Frog shrugged. 'More wine?' he asked.
'No thanks, I've had enough.'
'You are a horser,' the Frog reminded her gravely, as he got up to clear away their plates. 'You merst sterp being so afraid erf halcoherl.'
'I'm not afraid of alcohol,' Zoe snapped back and went off to her room.

Her head had begun to throb. She gazed at the exercise bike standing at the foot of her bed. 'Tomorrow,' she decided, and began unpacking her sheets. The thought of making the bed was too much. She decided to have a shower first. Taking her toilet bag, she walked slowly along the hall. God, she was tired. And she had forgotten how basic the bathroom was.

The bath was claw-footed and needed a good scrub.

She found the dark-green tiles on the wall depressing. As she stepped into the shower, two of the tiles fell off the wall onto the floor and broke, and a skink dropped from the ceiling onto her head. She turned on the taps and the pipes shrieked and groaned in protest. There was no soap.

When Zoe got out of the shower she still felt exhausted. Too late, she remembered she had forgotten to bring a towel. She couldn't even borrow the Frog's, because he didn't seem to have one either. Both the towel rails were empty. Then she saw the French flag furled up behind the door. Beyond caring how it got there, she wrapped the flag around herself and left her toilet bag sitting in the bath. Tomorrow she'd clear herself some space in the bathroom cupboard, which the Frog had filled with nail scissors, nail clippers, more empty toothpaste tubes, razor blades, boxes of herrings, a tube of some kind of anti-fungal cream which she didn't want to investigate too closely, and, mystifyingly, a map of Guadeloupe—the West Indies one. She returned to her room, curled up on the mattress, and fell fast asleep.

When Zoe awoke some hours later, the Frog and the cat were sitting at the foot of the bed, their noses in a book. Raising herself on her elbow she tried to see the title. It was M. F. K. Fisher's *With Bold Knife and Fork*.

'Oh, a cooking book,' she murmured, losing interest.

'Allo,' said the Frog, turning around. 'I see you berrowed my berth twirl.'

'I didn't borrow your bath towel. I borrowed the French flag.'

'That's wert I mean. I like you hin my berth twirl. I find you very sexy.'

'By the way,' said Zoe, 'why is there a map of Guadeloupe in the bathroom cupboard?'

'Bercurse I erlways wernted to go to Guadeloupe,' he replied. 'It wers a dream erf mine hin the seventies. I sterdy the map when I ham sitting ern the toilet.'

'It's not the seventies any longer,' said Zoe heartlessly.

'Do you ave to remind me, Zoe?'

Ignoring the Ayatollah, who was lying on its back and surveying her out of half-closed eyes, Zoe got up off the bed. 'What time is it?'

'Erlmost six hoclerk,' the Frog replied. 'I made you a leetle snerk.' He handed her a roasted capsicum stuffed with wild rice and herbs.

'How very thoughtful of you. Is this *the* capsicum?' Zoe added, as she took a bite.

The Frog nodded with a slightly martyred look. 'Oui, I sacrificed my leetle capsicerm jerst fur you.'

'Never mind,' said Zoe. 'Plenty more capsicums where this one came from.'

'Non, Zoe, this wern wers hunique.'

'Well, it's very good. I seem to have done nothing but eat since I got here.' The Frog beamed, but stopped when she added, 'I'd better have a food-free day tomorrow.'

'A wert?' he asked, mystified.

'Like a fast.'

'A wert?'

'It doesn't matter,' said Zoe, opening her suitcase and rifling through it for one of her sarongs.

'I ham going to wertch the two fat ladies ern TV,' the Frog announced. 'Werd you like to wertch it with me?'

'Yes, okay.'

'Bon!' he said. 'The Hayatollah and I will be waiting for you hin the living room.'

Zoe removed the French flag and hung it over her windowsill. Then she re-wrapped herself in a sarong, and stood for a moment by the window, watching as a long, narrow cargo ship, with Hong Kong markings on its hull, headed down the harbour towards the open sea. She wondered about the possibility of including a Hong Kong sea captain somewhere in her novel—he would have to be a Melville reader, of course.

Shouting started coming from the living room. Zoe walked in and saw the Frog having some kind of fit. Clutching her hand, he gestured wildly towards the TV set. 'Lerk, Zoe! This is ow we sherd heat, hinstead erf sterving hourselves to death! Lerts erf buttaire! Lerts erf hoil! Lerts erf crem! Ah oui, ah oui, ah oui! I sink I am going to hexplode, jerst watching them cerking ern the screen!'

He carried on in much the same vein throughout the rest of the program, and was completely worn out by the time it ended. 'Those two merst ave French blerd. They cennert be Hanglo-Saxons!' he said hoarsely, getting up to fetch some wine. Zoe switched to SBS to watch the news.

'Wert's appening?' said the Frog a minute later.

'The French and the English are fighting over beef again.'

'Perfidious Halbion!' roared the Frog. 'Nussing hever changes! That's why we can nevaire ave the Huropean Hunion!'

'Do you mind not shouting? I'm trying to listen to what they're saying,' said Zoe, exasperated. But the Frog, exercising his right as a Frenchman to defend his country at all costs, was off—howling that the English were all mad, and how the French were the only nation capable of keeping civilisation afloat.

Zoe switched the television off.

'Why did you do that, Zoe?' asked the Frog, pausing for breath.

'Because there's no point my trying to listen to the news when you're screaming your head off.'

'In that case, let's wertch the wildlife program,' cried

the Frog, taking control of the remote. 'I lerve the wildlife program! I wertch it hevery week! Where's the Hayatollah? E lerves the wildlife program too!'

'I bet it does,' muttered Zoe sourly. She turned in time to see the cat pad into the room. It sat down on a cushion on the floor, and fixed its eyes onto the TV screen, its tail flicking back and forth.

'C'est mignon, the leetle hole!' cried the Frog, in raptures next to her. 'Lerk! The leetle hole as cert a mousse!'

Zoe looked at the TV, and saw a small white owl chomping away at something with a long brown tail.

'Not mousse—mouse,' she said.

'Ow I lerve the way e heats!' moaned the Frog, as the owl shovelled another small rodent down its throat. The Ayatollah, on its cushion, let out a little growl.

'And now, ere cerms the sea hegel!' gasped the Frog. 'E his going to caught is dinner! Wertch!' The picture on the screen changed to show a baby iguana scrambling along a beach towards some rocks. 'E'll nevaire make hit!' screamed the Frog with joy, as an ominous shadow fell across the sand.

'Quick, little iguana! Run for your life!' cried Zoe, becoming involved, despite herself, in the wildlife drama.

'Erry erp!' bellowed the Frog at the sea eagle. 'Dinner his hescaping!'

At the very last moment the iguana reached the rocks and slipped under the biggest boulder. Just ahead of the sea eagle's talons. 'Oh, thank God!' exclaimed Zoe.

'We'll see,' replied the Frog. He watched the screen without moving a muscle. A moment later, the iguana, foolishly tempting fate, wriggled back out from under the rock. 'Oui!' roared the Frog, as the talons struck. 'Bravo! Encore!' He and the Ayatollah exchanged triumphant glances.

'Remind me never to watch a wildlife program with you again,' snapped Zoe.

'Bouf! That higuana ad a stupid face hanyway,' the Frog retorted.

The atmosphere was cool for the next hour or so—the Frog wisely occupying himself in the kitchen, while Zoe sat out on the balcony reading *Crime and Punishment*. At one point, the cry of seagulls made her glance up, just in time to see a crackle of pale green lightning.

'I think we're going to have one of Sydney's famous electrical storms,' she commented, as the Frog came out to join her. 'We don't often get them at this time of year. They can be quite spectacular.'

The two of them watched as the lightning continued, one moment green, the next moment a shocking Schiaparelli pink, zig-zagging across the pale, metal-coloured sky.

'If I'm away at the end of summer I miss the skies, those long-haul travellers of skies,' quoted Zoe.

'That's nice, Zoe.'

'Marguerite Duras,' Zoe answered.

'Do you hever terk habout hanysing hexcept literature?'

'Do you ever talk about anything *hexcept* food?'

'Speaking erf food,' said the Frog, 'I sink the feesh soup is erlmost ready.'

It was. The Frog handed her a glass of champagne and announced it was his birthday.

'You should have told me!' Zoe exclaimed. 'I would have bought you a birthday present.'

'You being ere his my present,' the Frog simpered. 'Bert I can sink erf ha very spesherl present, Zoe, hif you're hinterested.'

'Don't start,' she sighed.

'Hokay, I won't,' he promised. 'I'll be patient. Ow erld are you, Zoe?'

'Oh, you know, in my thirties.'

'And you aven't perblished a berk befur?'

'I wasn't *ready* to publish a book before. Unlike most writers, commercial success isn't the most important thing to me. I was more concerned with *writing* the book. Now, however, I'm prepared to contemplate the advantages of publishing.' Anxious to get off the subject of her age, she said, 'I'll take you out for dinner next week for your birthday.'

'I werd like that very merch, heven though I know I cerd cerk sermsing merch bettaire ere. Do you like my feesh soup?'

'It's absolutely delicious,' Zoe answered. And then added politely, 'How do you make it?'

'Ow I like,' replied the Frog, imperious again. 'First, I make a feesh sterk with feesh-heads and bones. This his very himpertant. Then I cerk serm mere feesh, pert it hin the sterk, and let hit simmer fur six or seven minutes. Then I pert han honion, a tomato, serm garlic and maybe serm celery, hinto a pan, and cerk it hinto a perlp. Then I pert the mixture through a sieve hinto my sterk. Voila! I make the garlic crouterns hat the lerst moment.'

'Is that an orthodox French recipe?' Zoe inquired.

'Bouf! That's ow *I* make hit, and that's wert's himperternt!'

Warming to this theme, he launched into a long dissertation on how courage in cooking—that is, opening a bottle of wine and improvising as you go—often brings brilliant results, as, he pointed out, he had demonstrated to Zoe that very night. He continued to labour this point over the creme caramels, which *were* heavenly. After singing 'The Marseillaise' twice and drinking a great deal of red wine—'Bert hit's my berthday, Zoe!'—he started to rave yet again about the Napoleonic Wars.

Zoe got up from the table. Birthday or no birthday, it was after midnight, and she had had enough. 'Goodnight,' she said, from the doorway.

The Frog's voice choked with emotion.

'I ham hunique hin this werld. Nowern cerks like me. I ham going to dedicate my feesh soup to Rabelais. E erlways ad the right hideas. E hand me—wert a cerperl we werd ave made!'

The next morning Zoe woke at 6 a.m., spent fifteen minutes on her exercise bike, wound another sarong around herself and sat down in front of her laptop.

She had bought her sarongs in Ubud, Bali, where she had lived for three months in the eighties. She had gone to Bali in order to become the next Graham Greene, after deciding there was no point trying to be Marguerite Duras if she couldn't write in French. But she had arrived in Ubud during the season of the dragonflies and was so captivated by the huge, emerald and crimson creatures whirling around the house she had rented that she found it difficult to concentrate. Nevertheless, she set herself a target of a thousand words a day and got down to work, determined to ignore the dreamy scene of the Balinese moving through the paddy-fields in the distance, like miniature figures in a painting. By the end of the first month she had completed two sentences—after which she gave up entirely and spent the rest of her time there wrapped in sloth and her sarong. She had obviously not been ready to write a book. Her writing had still been at a formative stage, her writer's mind needing more time to absorb her life experiences—unlike now, thought Zoe, tapping away at her laptop. By 8 a.m., she had written an entire paragraph. A record!

She got up, stretched, and gazed at the harbour. The steel facade of the bridge appeared to be sprouting from the rooftops of Kirribilli. A church bell began to toll somewhere across the water, and a man came out of a boatshed at the side of the bay and stood there, listening.

In a cheerful mood, Zoe went out to the kitchen to make some coffee. The Frog stumbled in, looking like a man who has been crawling through the desert. His hair was sticking up in tufts, his face was blotchy, and his eyes were half-closed and caked with sand.

'I eard noises, so I came to hinvestigate,' he croaked, clutching at a tiny red kimono, covered in a garish parrot print, which he had pulled around himself. 'Wert are you doing ere hin the middle erf the night?'

'It's past eight o'clock and I need coffee,' Zoe answered, averting her eyes from his near-nudity. The kimono was ridiculously undersized. Was he wearing it on purpose? She decided it was probably Ziggi's. 'I assume it is okay for me to make coffee,' she said sarcastically.

'Erp to a point,' replied the Frog. He started limping around the kitchen, groaning, and said piteously, 'My fert his urting me.'

Zoe gave it a cursory glance. 'It looks fine to me. A bit puffy, perhaps. Would you like some coffee?'

'I cannert drink ot coffee,' mourned the Frog. 'Hit burns my tongue. I ave to wait huntil hit's cerld.' He started poking around in the fridge. 'There's nevaire hanysing to heat hin these ouse,' he grumbled, pulling out the remains of a lentil stew, a roasted poussin he had forgotten about, cheese, grapes, tomatoes, the rest of the leek soup, an extra creme caramel which he had hidden behind the olives and a slice of onion tart. 'I serperse that will ave to do,' he said, leaving the tart and the lentil stew on the table and putting everything else back.

'For breakfast?' Zoe asked in amazement.

'Oui. Why nert? It's food, hisn't hit? Werd you like serm?'

'No thanks. I rarely eat breakfast. Sometimes a piece of fruit. There aren't any bananas, are there? Oh God—I'm sorry.'

'That's hokay,' sighed the Frog. 'I try nert to sink habout my youth hany mere.'

'What's that smell?' Zoe asked suddenly, staring around the kitchen.

'Wert smell?'

'I can't explain. It seems to come and go. I noticed it last night.'

The Frog sniffed the air extravagantly. 'I cannert smell hanysing, Zoe. You sherd go and werk ern your noverl, hinstead erf chatting hin the kitchen. I do nert wernt you distracted by ferny smells er hanysing helse.'

'Yes, okay,' said Zoe, touched by his thoughtfulness. 'See you later on.' She took her coffee and returned to her room.

An hour later a frenzied yelling started in the distance. 'What now?' muttered Zoe, getting to her feet. She went and hovered in the vestibule. 'What's the matter?' she called out.

'The bluddy sings keep getting hin my way! I wish I cerd pert them hin a drawer!'

'What do you wish you could put in a drawer?'

'My balls!' the Frog shouted, appearing in the hall in his underpants.

Zoe blinked and looked away. He was doing it on purpose! 'Did your underpants shrink in the wash?' she asked, as delicately as she could.

'My hunderpants erlways shrink hin the wersh! Soon,

I ham going to sterp wearing them herltogether! I ate aving to pert ern clothes! Erl those berttons ern my shirt I ave to do erp! Wert an hidiotic waste erf time!'

'I thought you weren't going to interrupt me when I write. You've ruined my train of thought. I was reworking the narrative in a new direction, and now I can't remember what it was I was trying to achieve!' snapped Zoe. 'I may as well have a shower and then try to start again.'

'I ad my shower erlready,' the Frog said with some pride. 'Do you wernt to sniff me? I smell absolutely deevine. I ferned serm perfume hin your toilet bag, and I pert hit hin my hermpits, and sermwhere helse I don't sink I sherd tell you habout.'

'That perfume costs a fortune!' Zoe cried, outraged.

'Erf curse hit cerst a furtune! Hit's French!' the Frog replied. He turned around and arched his back. 'Do you sink my berm's too big?'

The Frog had left a cake of his precious Marseilles soap in the bathroom. She was soaping herself in the shower, when he stuck his head around the door and offered to scrub her back. 'Go away!' Zoe ordered him, aware that he was studying her silhouette in the steamed-up glass doors. He left her in peace, and when she emerged from the bathroom he was nowhere to be seen.

At 11 a.m., as she was trying to locate the right place for a comma in the paragraph she had written earlier that morning, the door to her room was shoved open and the Frog staggered in and fell on the bed. 'I ham hin hexcruciating pain!' he howled.

'How dare you keep doing this to me!' Zoe responded. 'I knew moving in here was a mistake! Joan Didion would never have been talked into it. Do you know what really gets on my nerves? The way my creative tension as a writer is being pushed into the background by your ongoing existential despair!'

'Bert Zoe, lerk hat my fert!' bellowed the Frog. 'It's erl swerllen herp. It's like a rottern hegg-plernt. I dern't care habout aving herngoing hexistential despair! I ham hin hagony!'

Zoe glanced at the foot and was startled by its angry, purplish-red appearance. 'It looks dreadful,' she agreed, then turned back to the computer. 'What do you expect me to do about it?' she asked, staring at the screen again. No, that comma would have to go.

'I wernt you to drive me to the ospiterl,' moaned the Frog. 'I erlready telephoned my specialist, and terld him to get hin there hern the derble. Hunless you cerd ring your father hinstead.'

'I told you, he's a gynaecologist, and anyway, my parents are overseas,' said Zoe.

'Elp me! Ow can I get to ospiterl when I can ardly stand erp?'

'Great!' said Zoe. 'Just when I was finally able to concentrate on the manneristic nuances in my paragraph. I may as well ring Ian and tell him he can forget about publishing my book, because I'm never going to be able to finish it!'

'I dern't care habout your perblisher, e dersn't make the dinner,' whimpered the Frog. 'I sink my fert his going to drerp erf. We ad bettaire go right haway.'

In the car the Frog stretched out on the back seat, wailing, further aggravating Zoe's nerves. She became even more furious when he told her they weren't going to the Royal North Shore Hospital, as she had expected, but to the Prince of Wales Hospital, in Randwick. 'But that's on the other side of the city,' she cried.

'I know, bert that's where my specialist his,' he gasped, between moans. 'It's wern erf the best ospiterls hin Sydney. And hanyway, they know me there.'

Sure enough, the staff in the accident and emergency clinic greeted the Frog like an old and valued friend. As he encouraged them to exclaim in horror at his foot, his eyes alighted on a nurse he had never seen before. 'Are you pert erf my medicerl team?' he inquired.

The nurse, who had the most gorgeous cheekbones Zoe had ever seen, replied, 'Oui, I am Mernique, the sister hin charge. The specialist will be ere hany minute.'

'You're French!' cried the Frog in ecstasy, as Zoe groaned. 'Which pert erf France are you frem?'

'Paris,' Monique told him.

'Same ere,' said the Frog, before giving another sudden shriek of anguish. He toppled over into her arms.

'This man,' announced Monique, as an orderly rushed to help them up from the floor, 'is hextremely brave. I hexpect heverywern to hassist him hin hany way e wernts.'

'I need a trelley,' barked the Frog. 'I ave to rest. And lerts erf pillows. And a blankert to keep my fert werm. And do you sink I cerd ave sermsing to heat, to keep herp my strength?'

'They've got chicken waldorf salad in the canteen,' the orderly suggested.

'That will ave to do, I serppose, although I might need a bedpern hafterwerds,' replied the Frog. 'Cerd I ave a head and neck massage while I wait?'

Monique snapped her fingers at a serious-looking young nurse in her twenties. 'Get the chicken waldorf salad,' she ordered.

'Right away!' replied nurse number two, and rushed off down the corridor. Zoe watched with disbelief as Monique massaged the Frog with perfectly manicured fingers, murmuring little endearments to him in their own language.

'Oooh, oui, c'est superb,' breathed the Frog, adding

in English by mistake, 'you can go further down hif you wernt.'

'Sssh,' said Monique. 'Try to relax. You're very tense.'

'I sink I need serm morphine,' the Frog suggested.

She chuckled. 'Dern't be nerty.'

'I ham a very nerty boy,' the Frog agreed. 'Cerdn't you steal serm morphine frem hanother werd?' he persisted.

Douglas Epsom, the specialist, appeared. He was a man of around fifty, with a beard and tired eyes.

'Bonjour, Monsieur Frog!' said Dr Epsom, stealing a piece of celery from the salad which had just arrived. 'Not more beetroot stains, I hope?'

The Frog threw him a reproachful glance. 'Show him,' he said to Monique.

'Good heavens,' responded the specialist, astonished, as Monique removed the blanket from the foot. 'How on earth did it get like that? We'd better X-ray it straight away.'

'This is honly the beginning,' moaned the Frog, then cried out in pain.

'The beginning of what?' asked Dr Epsom, still hovering over the foot.

'The beginning erf the hend—when erl my bits and pieces stert ferlling erf!'

'Cheer up!' Zoe called out to him, as the Frog was wheeled away, still bellowing out his bleak prognosis. 'Just eat some garlic and spontaneously combust!'

'That wers nert very nice,' Monique rebuked Zoe. 'Dern't you ave hany cermpassion fur the poor man?' She hurried off after her patient, and Zoe, with a sigh of relief, sat down and start rereading the 1991 issue of *Granta* with 'Vargas Llosa for President' on the cover. She was lost on the campaign trail with Vargas Llosa in Peru, when Dr Epsom returned and asked her if she would mind keeping the Frog company. 'We've done the X-ray, but there's a bit of a delay before his foot can be properly examined,' he explained. 'We've got a suspected suicide attempt in the queue ahead of him, and Monsieur Frog is furious about having to wait.'

'Surprise, surprise,' said Zoe, getting up and following the specialist down the corridor. 'Will you have to keep him in overnight?' she asked with a sudden surge of hope.

'Oh, I don't think so. With luck you'll be able to take him home this afternoon,' Dr Epsom replied, adding, 'He tells me you're writing a novel. He's in luck. That means you'll have all the time in the world to nurse him back to health.'

'Absolutely,' Zoe agreed. 'Chekhov used to give pedicures to the deaf and dumb in his spare time.'

'Is that so?' said Dr Epsom. 'Well, here we are. Monsieur Frog is just through those swing-doors over there.'

Zoe walked through to find the Frog reclining like

one of the twelve Caesars on his trolley, surrounded by a group of earnest Chinese students. Monique, who was standing guard, was explaining to the Frog that the students had come from Hong Kong and were keen to watch the examination.

'I dern't mind, as lerng as they tell me ow to make shark fin soup,' the Frog whimpered on his pillows. He turned his head as the suicide attempt was pushed past him. 'Why don't you let the hidiot die, hif that's wert he wernts?' he bellowed. 'I ham hin mere pain than e his!'

Catching sight of Zoe, he started giving heart-breaking little yelps. 'I'm nert aving a good time hat erl,' he told her, looking so tragic that she almost believed him. 'The chicken waldorf salad wers habsolutely dersgersting! Arrrrgggggh!' he screamed, clutching her arm. 'Why can't hanywern do hanysing fur me? Do I ave to hamputate my fert myself?'

His screams brought medical staff from several specialties running into the examination room, and soon there were a dozen men and women in white coats standing around the trolley with the Chinese students. 'It looks like gout,' remarked a rheumatologist, peering at the Frog's blighted foot. 'A blood test should confirm it.'

'Gout?' howled the Frog. 'Ow cerd I ave gout? That's han Hanglo-Saxon disease! I find this a totally hern-reasonaberl diagnersis! Jerst like my igh cholesterol!'

'Are you a big drinker?' the rheumatologist inquired.

'Mais non!' the Frog protested. 'I ave a glass ere and there—nert has merch has serm peoperl. I feel like a glass erf red wine now, as a matter erf fact.'

'Sorry,' said Dr Epsom. 'I can't allow it.'

'Why nert?' the Frog demanded. 'Why is there erlways sermwern telling me wert I can and cannert do? Why can I nevaire do wert I wernt? I erlways knew my life werd be a nightmare. It sterted when my trempert ferll to pieces at the village concert.'

'My little brother bashed *my* trumpet over my head when I was little,' recalled an ENT surgeon, whose white coat didn't quite disguise the brief singlet-dress she was wearing underneath. 'I never forgot it, either.'

'Chilherds are erlferl, aren't they?' the Frog commiserated with her. 'You ave very nice calves,' he added. 'I noticed them befur.' He pulled out a cigarette and lit it.

Monique snatched the cigarette away. 'That's very bad fur your ealth,' she scolded him. 'We Heuropeans, we perff haway like chimneys. We ave to sterp.'

'We know there is nussing hin life to lerk furwerd to,' the Frog reminded her. 'That is why we be'ave the way we do. We're erl doomed,' he continued, raising his voice. 'Lerk hat my fert. Next, I hexpect it will be my teeth—and then wert, I wernder?'

'Don't even think about it,' a urologist called out from the back of the room.

A physician friend of Dr Epsom's, who had come to give a second opinion about the foot—he also thought it looked like gout—patted the Frog's shoulder reassuringly. 'Don't be so pessimistic,' he said. 'These problems you're having with your health are fixable.'

'Honly by death,' came the bitter reply.

The physician exchanged a look with Dr Epsom, as if to say, 'glad he's your patient and not mine' and glanced at his watch. 'Well, I must be off,' he said. 'I've got a hip replacement to do in half an hour.'

'Han ip replacement?' the Frog said chattily. 'Bouf! Erl your patient needs his serm rabbit cerked hin red wine. A Côtes-du-Rhône will do. Bert you ave to remember to marinate the rabbit hin the wine fur at least twenty-four hours. Hanglo-Saxons ave no hidea. They sink hanysing that takes lernger than ten minutes to cerk is fureign merk. You merst huse wine vinegar and hunpeeled garlic hin the marinade, avec horegano, bay leaf, thyme and crecked peppercorns. And you merst huse holive hoil. This is merst himpertant!'

'Thank you,' the physician replied, as the Chinese students wrote it all down in their notepads. 'That sounds like a bloody good recipe. But,' the physician continued, 'your view of Anglo-Saxon cooking is outdated. Cooking has really taken off in this country. Sydney now has some of the finest restaurants in the world.'

'Ah, oui, wern er two,' the Frog conceded. 'Bert people still dern't heat enerf leek soup. Hit's becurse they dern't heat leek soup that they ferll hover—and then you hend erp doing ip replacements erl day lerng.'

'An interesting theory,' the physician commented. 'I'll talk to the hospital nutritionist. And now I really must be off. Take care of that foot. Perhaps you should give rich food a miss for a while.'

'I nevaire heat rich food!' the Frog protested. 'I heat hextremely lightly. You sherd try my derk liver, perk and veal terrine!' The physician stretched his lips into the smile he kept for patients suffering dementia, and bolted.

Zoe brushed past Monique and approached the orator on his trolley. 'If you've quite finished lecturing everyone, I'd like to go home and get back to my book,' she told him.

'Yes, I think that's in order,' said Dr Epsom. 'Here are some pain-killers to help you through the rest of the afternoon, and I want you to start taking these as well,' he said, handing the Frog some anti-gout pills. 'And drink lots and lots of water. This is essential.'

'Werter?' shouted the Frog. 'I nevaire drink werter! I really cannert do this! You are hasking the himperssiberl!'

'You must,' said Dr Epsom firmly.

A flotilla of nurses, with Monique at their head,

accompanied the Frog to the hospital entrance, applauding him as he hauled himself along on the crutches provided, chewing on his pain-killers.

'I suppose you expect me to make dinner tonight,' said Zoe, as she drove the Peugeot back to Neutral Bay. 'I knew your cooking routine was just a ruse.'

'Herf curse I dern't hexpect you to cerk dinner,' the Frog replied. 'I made a coq au vin this merning, befur my fert blew erp.'

'Speaking of food, some of us haven't had a single thing to eat today. We've been too busy running after other people. I'll grab some lunch here,' said Zoe, stopping outside a delicatessen. 'Do you want anything?'

'Non, I'll heat the leetle poussin when we get ome,' the Frog replied, swallowing another pain-killer. 'Wert did you buy?' he asked, the moment Zoe got back into the car. 'Let me see,' he said, trying to grab the paper bag she was holding.

'Leave me alone! You don't own my appetite, you know,' she retorted.

'Oui, I do,' the Frog replied. 'Hanglo-Saxons ave to be kept hunder surveillance erl the time.'

Outside the apartment, he watched with astonishment as Zoe's key slid easily into the door. 'Why dersn't mine hever do that?' he said, hobbling after her as she walked into the kitchen. Zoe opened the deli bag, took out two samosas and a small baguette, and picked up a fork. 'I cannert believe wert I ham seeing!' screamed the Frog, as she began mashing the samosas onto the baguette. 'Sterp this hatrocity hat wernce!'

'Oh, don't be so old-fashioned,' Zoe answered. 'Arundhati Roy, Salman Rushdie, Vikram Seth and Amitav Ghosh have changed the face of English literature, so why not apply the same principle to food? Or don't you like Indian cuisine?'

'I lerve Indian cuisine, bert that his nert the point! You cannert pert a samosa hon a baguette! I will nert tolerate this hanarchy. I'm werning you, Zoe.' He limped out of the kitchen into the living room, where he sat down heavily on the sofa, arranging himself so that his foot rested on a cushion, and proceeded to furiously mutter to himself in French.

After finishing her lunch, Zoe took a large glass of water to him. He looked at her with such an ominous expression that she began to wonder if she really had gone too far. 'You have to drink a lot of water,' she said tentatively, 'so you may as well start now.'

The Frog screwed up his face, took a few sips and shuddered as if he had just swallowed a mouthful of petrol. Ignoring his dramatics, Zoe put another cushion behind his head, and brought the phone over to the side of the sofa. 'I'm going to write. I'll leave my mobile on. You can ring me if you need anything,' she said.

'Hokay,' he said stonily.

'Do you want the poussin on a plate with some grapes?'

'Hafter wert you jerst did hin the kitchen, I ave lerst my happetite cermpletely.'

'Well then, is there anything else you need?'

'A dry mertini werd be nice.'

'Do you think that's wise?'

'Oui.'

'On top of pain-killers?'

'Oui.'

'Do you have any gin and vermouth in the house?'

'Oui.'

'Oh, well,' Zoe sighed. 'You have had a rough day.'

'Why dern't you ave a mertini too, Zoe?'

'Because they go straight to my head,' Zoe answered.

'Do they really?' asked the Frog, brightening. 'Ow hinteresting. And yet Proust erlways had a leetle mertini befur sitting down to write.'

'Did he?' said Zoe uncertainly. 'Well, perhaps I could have just one. It's been a tiring day for me as well.' She went to fetch some glasses.

'You see?' said the Frog a short time later, as they sat in the living room, sipping their drinks. 'Hisn't hit refreshing?'

'Yes, it is,' said Zoe, surprised at how good the martini tasted. She took another sip. The next thing she was aware of was her mobile ringing. She tried to sit up, failed, and realised she was lying on the floor. She crawled across the room, feeling her way over to the phone. 'Yes?' she said hoarsely.

'Wert are you doing?' inquired a voice, which also seemed to emanate from somewhere close by. Through blurred vision, she could just make out the Frog wallowing on the sofa.

'What's going on?' she slurred.

'Zoe! I sink you're serzzled!'

'I told you I couldn't drink martinis,' she moaned.

'Bouf! You ernly ad wern,' said the Frog in derision. 'Wern mertini and you're ern your nerse.'

'I had three. You had fallen asleep!'

'It merst ave been the pain-killer I terk. Why did you ave tree martinis, Zoe?'

She began to sob. Her head was thumping. 'Because I'll never write like Milan Kundera!'

The Frog picked up his crutches and pulled himself off the sofa. Swaying slightly, but otherwise managing to remain upright, he announced, 'You know, herf curse, that Kundera became a French citizen serm time hago. Wert a sensiberl man. I like Kundera very merch. E wernce said that life his a trap we've erlways known, that we're bern without being hasked, we're lerked hin a berdy we nevaire chose, and we're desturned to die. Hexactly wert I ave been saying erl halerng! There's no ope.'

Zoe hauled herself across the floor to the vacated

sofa, and fell face-down onto the cushions. 'Poor Zoe. Werd you like me to hundress you, so you can breathe mere heasily?'

'I might have known you'd try to take advantage of the situation,' Zoe hiccuped, rolling over. 'I just need to rest. I'm having a literary crisis, that's all.'

'The French nevaire take hadvantage herf wormen when they are drunk,' the Frog reprimanded her. 'In fact, we don't take hadvanatage erf wormen hat erl. They take hadvantage erf us, and we are too polite to refuse.'

'I'm not drunk.'

'Herf curse you are, Zoe. You're a writer! I wers getting werried.'

'I'm so glad I'm not such a hopeless, literary letdown after all.'

'Termerrow you will be very angry. I will leave serm coq au vin fur your lernch. Bert it will be the lerst time you henter the kitchen freely.'

Zoe's eyes creaked open. 'What are you talking about?' she said.

'You'll see,' said the Frog. 'You brert it ern yourself.' He sounded almost sorrowful.

'It's because of the samosas, isn't it?'

There was no reply. With a huge effort, Zoe opened her eyes again. The Frog was gone.

At 5 a.m., the harbour was a rich, lapis lazuli blue.

Wincing at the martini tide now reduced to rockpools in her brain, Zoe tiptoed through the apartment to make some coffee. The Frog would never be up so early. Sure enough, there was no one in the kitchen and she wasted no time turning on the kettle. Her nose twitched. There was that strange smell again. What *was* it? Rather than investigate, she went straight back to her room once the coffee was ready. The sooner she resumed writing, the better—especially after yesterday. She had to make up for lost time.

Ian, her publisher, had left a message on the answering machine reminding her to bring the first six chapters to their lunch, a few days away. The problem was, by reconceptualising the narrative yet again, she'd had to delete chapters one to five. Still, now that she had sorted out the comma problem in the paragraph written the previous day, she should be able to move on briskly without any more interruptions—although she half hoped Ian would ring and disturb her. She liked being disturbed by her publisher while she was working. It proved she was a writer. She switched on her mobile in anticipation.

At 8 a.m., after writing a single sentence, deleting it, rewriting it, then sticking it in yesterday's paragraph to see if it worked better there, she made a return trip to the kitchen for more coffee. She could hardly believe her luck. The Frog must still be out cold. She had thought she heard a floorboard creaking earlier on, but must have imagined it. She wondered briefly if he had overdosed on the pain-killers, but decided not to check to see whether he had. Two interruptions to her writing in two days would be too much.

At 9 a.m., her mobile began to ring. 'Oh good,' said Zoe.

'Merde!' screamed a voice down the line. 'That's the treberl with the hocean! Hit has too many waves!'

Zoe heard seagulls in the background, and then the sound of surf. 'Where are you?' she asked.

'Hat the beach! I crept hout erf the ouse like a leetle mousse, so that I werd nert disturb you. Writers need solertude. I hundersternd this completely! I wers piddling hin the shallows hin my shirts, when I erlmost got wershed away! Ow ham I meant to piddle when I ham ern crertches? Now my shirts are wet, and I will ave pimperls hon my berm termerrow,' the Frog added piteously.

'I do hope when you say piddle, you mean paddle,' Zoe commented. 'And your shorts should dry in five minutes in this heat. When will you be back?'

'Nert huntil merch later,' the Frog replied. 'I ham taking Ziggi's merld to han hartist friend's studio, to see wert e sinks erf it. Then I'm aving lernch with Ziggi. She wernts to see er merld.'

'Doesn't she have to practise her scales or something?' said Zoe, a bit miffed at all this fuss over some concert pianist's perfectly ordinary fingers.

'I ave to take a merld erf er shurlders. She cermissioned me. It's a present fur er ersband.'

'Oh, she has a husband, does she?'

'Dern't furget you've got coq au vin fur lernch. I've left you writtern hinstrections habout ow to turn ern the hervern. I'll buy serm pate de foie gras fur a leetle treat tonight.'

'You're not meant to be eating rich food, remember.'

'Pate de foie gras his nert rich food. Honly han

Hanglo-Saxon cerd say a sing like that. Pate de foie gras hincreases the circulation and gets rid herf varicerse veins. Please dern't bern the coq au vin, Zoe,' he went on. 'Coq au vin his very himpertant to me. I ham sad I wern't be there to see you heat hit. I'll make a lemern souffle when I get berk.'

'I can't wait,' said Zoe, hanging up. She stared at the paragraph on the laptop. She hated it. Worse, it made no sense. It was all the Frog's fault for ringing her. How could anyone understand anything after one of his telephone calls? Perhaps some imagery would make her sentence clearer. Zoe got up from her desk and walked through into the living room. She took Nabokov's *Lolita* from the shelves, and flicked through the opening pages. Nabokov did brilliant imagery: 'a blue-sea wave swelled under my heart'. Why couldn't she write words like that—especially with a harbour view? She'd pinch the line and add it to the paragraph. Nabokov wouldn't have minded, she was sure. Writers had to help each other out.

How quiet it was in the apartment without the Frog. Zoe decided to power-walk around the apartment in order to get her literary imagination really going. She *could* write while sitting on her exercise bike of course, but it had her Tom Wolfe collection balanced on the seat.

A ray of sunlight fell over the secretaire, and the

poignant photograph, framed in black, of the Frog sitting on his potty. Zoe picked it up and studied it, struck, once again, by the expression on his face. How was it possible for a toddler to look both so cantankerous and so world-weary? She checked her watch. There was plenty of time to rifle through the secretaire's drawers before the Frog got home. She told herself she was only looking after her interests. Who knew what murky secrets he was hiding from his past? Perhaps she'd get a new idea for her novel.

In the small drawer at the top she found bills, postcards, an old ivory cigarette case and a copy of Molière's *Le Malade Imaginaire*. In the second drawer, she found more postcards, pens, a sock and a jar of gherkins. In the third there was nothing except a blue and red checked tea towel, knotted at the top.

Zoe picked it up and a letter slipped from its folds and fell onto the floor. She reached down to retrieve it, and saw that it had been written by Denise, the Frog's grandmother, and that it was dated twenty-four years earlier. 'Damn!' Zoe muttered. She could read French, after a fashion, but not well enough to be sure she could understand every phrase. Then she saw that each page was followed by another page translated into English— courtesy of the local schoolteacher, according to a postscript. Separating the English pages from the French, Zoe sat down on the sofa, and was soon absorbed in the day-to-day life of the lost village in the Vandee countryside, where the Frog spent his early childhood. His grandmother wrote simply and movingly of her grandson's formative years. Her letter was a memoir which, as she explained, she hoped would double as a form of diplomatic immunity.

'I told him to keep this letter in his passport and not to lose it no matter where he goes. Today, you see, my grown-up grandson is going out into the world to try to find the reason for his existence. He's carrying nothing but a 750 gram can of pure melted goose fat, a corkscrew, a vegetable peeler and some goose-giblet stew in a jar with its lid screwed tightly on.

'My grandson has very strong opinions about everything, and believes wholeheartedly that mankind is cursed,' Denise wrote. 'Please go easy on him if he's carrying more cigarettes and alcohol than he should, and please do not confiscate his baby-teeth, which I have wrapped up and included with these pages. I want him to have a keepsake from his childhood.'

Zoe shook the other pages of the letter. No baby-teeth. Where were they? Had the Frog dropped them when crossing some border? She checked the folds of the red and blue checked tea towel. Nothing. She resumed reading.

'You may find that he complains about his childhood, but it wasn't as awful as he insists. I do wish he wouldn't keep going on about that worm in his bathwater. I told him that during the war we had to have cold baths, even in winter, but he said that wasn't the point.

'Perhaps we were wrong to tell him that all those photographs of Parisians dancing in the street, waving flags and kissing American soldiers, were of people celebrating his birth. He was just a little boy when we told him and I had no idea he would remember it. We were so shocked that day when he came home from school, sobbing that his heart was broken. I didn't know they taught six-year-olds about the liberation of France. I really do think they should wait until children are a little older…'

The minutes ticked away. The letter was a revelation. Zoe smelled the scent of rosemary and thyme growing in the herb garden outside the kitchen door, saw the Frog learning from his grandmother how to make coq au vin, and watched him as a small boy, going down to the river to sculpt women's bottoms out of mud. She understood now why the Frog had spoken with such emotion about coq au vin. It was the second dish his grandmother had ever taught him to cook, after leek soup. She put the letter in her pocket, went to the phone and called Howard.

'Zoe, I'm glad you called. I've been wondering how you and the Frog were getting along. I was hoping you could add to some notes I started making at Max and Madeleine's about his behaviour. He's a very interesting case.'

'As a matter of fact,' Zoe replied, 'there is something you should see. A letter written by his grandmother, Denise, which I found while I was tidying up the place. The only thing I can't find is the baby-teeth.'

'The baby-teeth?' said Howard.

'The Frog is out,' said Zoe, pushing on. 'He'll be back later. Can you come to lunch? It's coq au vin.'

'I love coq au vin!' Howard gushed. 'I'll cancel my patients and come over straight away.'

'Won't they mind? Your patients?'

'I'll tell them they have to learn to adjust to changes in routine. I'm sure they'll understand. I have their absolute trust.'

Zoe was turning on the oven (having carefully studied the Frog's instructions), when there was a noisy jangling of keys in the front door, followed by a familiar stream of curses. She jumped. What was the Frog doing home so early? It was only half past one.

'Hi,' she said, as calmly as she could, as he limped into the kitchen, holding onto the bench with his free hand. He was sporting a nautical look today—a dark blue T-shirt worn loose over the shorts which had had such a soaking earlier on. He still had sea-salt on his legs, she noticed.

'Soon, I ham going to demerlish that door!' said the Frog, thumping his shopping down onto the table.

'What happened? I thought you had an appointment with Tiggi.'

'Ziggi. She wers called haway to a rehearsal she ad forgottern habout. And we were going to ave schnapper pie fur lernch!'

'How nice,' said Zoe. 'A concert pianist who can cook. Why didn't she give you a slice of the pie to take with you?'

'She furgert! I'll nevaire furgive er!'

'And where are your crutches?'

'I threw them hin the hocean!'

'Of course. That makes sense. I hope you weren't intending to eat most of the coq au vin yourself, because Howard is coming over to lunch.'

'Bon! I'll hopern a nice berttle herf burgundy. Shranks erlways like a drink.'

Howard arrived a few minutes later. He wore a grey three-piece suit, with a 'Save the Penguins' button attached to his lapel. 'Antarctica makes me wear it,' he explained, looking a bit embarrassed. The button detracted from his James Joyce looks, Zoe noted with disapproval.

'The Frog's back,' she warned him sotto voce, handing him the letter with great stealth.

'I feel like a conspirator,' the psychiatrist joked, undoing the top two buttons of his shirt, the way he did with his more uptight patients.

Appropriately enough, lunch passed in whispers. The Frog ate, as usual, without speaking, and Zoe and Howard, not wishing to disturb him, conversed quietly.

'Be careful how you arrange your leftovers,' Zoe whispered in the psychiatrist's ear, as he finished speaking.

'I heard about the quail from Max,' he mumbled back.

'Feenished?' said the Frog suddenly, looking up from his plate. 'Werd you like serm mere?'

Before Zoe or Howard could reply, the Ayatollah came in from the balcony with half a goldfish in its mouth. Dropping the corpse at the Frog's feet, it took up its Bombay Begging Bowl position, spreadeagling itself on the floor, its breath coming in tiny short gasps as it stared imploringly at its benefactor.

'Heven sauteed, I dern't sink it will taste merch good,' the Frog broke the bad news to the Ayatollah, after picking up the goldfish remains. 'Better try the coq au vin hinstead. Zoe and Howard ave ad enerf, aven't you?'

'Oh. Yes, of course,' said Howard, who had just reached across the table to help himself to more. He withdrew his arm and smiled his professional smile.

'No,' said Zoe, at the same time.

The Frog, with his usual inattention to peripheral matters, got up from the table. 'Bon! Why dern't you sit hout ern the berlcony, while I give the chat is lernch? Then I'll make the lemern souffle fur dessert.'

'The balcony isn't a bad idea,' Zoe murmured to Howard, after she and the cat had exchanged baleful looks. 'You can sit out there and read the letter.'

Howard nodded, and took his reading glasses from his pocket. Luckily for them, the Frog was behaving quite normally, carrying on like a madman in the kitchen, dropping things and shouting.

'He seems to be doing a lot of drilling and banging for someone who's meant to be cooking a souffle,' Zoe commented as Howard bent over Denise's letter. 'I'll just go and see what he's doing.' A minute or so later, she returned, stunned, to the balcony. 'He's deadlocked the kitchen door!'

'I werned you habout your hatrocious be'aviour,' a voice thundered out the window. 'I can no lernger herllow you hin my kitchen ern your hown. Hanyway, I'm sinking habout my lemern souffle, and I dern't wernt to be disturbed—just like you dern't wernt to be disturbed when you are writing!'

'How can you even compare the two things?' Zoe yelled back.

'Zoe, don't make a fuss,' Howard hissed, getting out of his chair in such a hurry that he left the letter on the seat. 'You'll just have to accept the deadlock for the moment. It represents the key to the kingdom he never had as a child. Don't you understand?'

'Yes. It's pathetic,' said Zoe.

There was a sudden scream from the kitchen. 'Merde! My leetle souffle as cerllapsed!' The Frog rushed out onto the balcony, and threw his hands to the sky in the time-honoured way of people left with nothing after tidal waves and earthquakes. 'A disaster!' he shouted. 'A catastrophe!'

'Worse than Waterloo,' said Zoe. Howard shook his head at her, and with difficulty, she changed her tone. 'It's only a souffle. You can always make another one.'

'Non! Je refuse! I will let my souffle dry hinto a disc, and termerrow, I will throw hit around the garden like han hancient Greek. That his erl that I can do!' He put his face into his hands. 'Why ders nussing hever go right? I sink I ham losing my merble.'

'Marbles,' Zoe corrected him. 'It's plural.'

'Wern his quite henerf,' moaned the Frog, and went to sit down in Howard's chair. 'Wert his this?' he said, reaching for Denise's letter.

With an appalled look at Howard, Zoe took a couple of steps towards the Frog. She had to act quickly, otherwise he would assume he could also look through her things when she wasn't around. If he turned on her laptop, for example, and tried to read her novel, all would be lost. She could picture the scene—the Frog shouting the moment she got through the door, 'Bert Zoe, wert ders this mean? Hafter erl this time werking ern hour noverl, you ave ernly written five paragraphs?' Well, he was the one who said at Max and Madeleine's that it took writers years to produce anything because they didn't eat. She'd remind him of what he'd said. The problem was, she knew what his riposte would be. 'Bert Zoe! Now you are heating! I ham cerking erl the meals!'

Zoe knelt down beside the Frog and took his hands in hers. 'I'm so sorry,' she said. 'I was looking for, er, a stamp, and I happened to see the letter in the secretaire. I read it. I could not help it. I'm so fascinated by your life.'

'I like it when you old my ands, Zoe,' replied the Frog. 'Do you find me sexy?'

'So I rang Howard,' Zoe went on, 'because I thought he might be able to help you.'

'Elp me? Ow?'

'Childhood is a complex business,' explained Howard, coming to the rescue. 'I think there were things that upset you deeply when you were a child that were never resolved, and which still haunt you.'

'My feets herpset me,' the Frog agreed. 'They were the biggest feets hever seen ern a child hin France. Nern erf the herther childrens ad feets like mine. When I wers holder, and went swimming hin the river, I erlways kept my shoes ern, so the herther childrens werdn't laugh hat me.'

'I must admit, you do have big feet,' said Zoe without thinking. 'What size are they?'

'Size sirteen,' the Frog said despondently. 'I hused to wertch them grow while I wers setting ern my perty—and I know they're still growing. That's why I ave so many preblerms with them. I tried to tell Dr Hepsom this, bert has husual, no wern listens.'

'I understand you were quite advanced in other ways,' said Howard, trying to cheer him up. 'Your grandmother says you were five when you tried to have an affair with the young woman who worked in the village patisserie. You invited her to model naked for you.'

'She wers hokay—nussing special.'

'Weren't you intimidated by the age difference?' Howard persisted.

'Mais non,' scoffed the Frog. 'Hevery leetle boy hin France tries to make holder wormen get hundressed. It's like reading Victor Ugo—a rite erf passage.'

Zoe took the letter from the Frog before he could launch into a dissertation on the main preoccupation of French minors. 'When you were six, your grandmother took you to see an animated film.'

'Oui, I remember,' the Frog said with a heavy sigh.

'You were thrilled to be going to the cinema at last. You sat on the edge of your seat, your eyes fixed on the screen as the lights dimmed and the film began.

Glancing at your rapt profile, your grandmother saw that you had been transported into another world.'

'Ah yes!' Howard interjected. 'That's the point I mentally underlined before.'

'There was a beautiful princess in the movie who used to scatter chocolates in the forest for children who were lost. A prince fell in love with her, and kissed her behind a giant mushroom.'

'Is this all true?' asked Howard. 'I think I'm beginning to see the problem.'

'Oui,' the Frog said mournfully. 'It's hexactly has my grandmerther describes. She ad erlready taught me ow to make champignons a la bordelaise, so I knew that mershrerms did nert grow as big as that, and I nevaire saw hany chocolates hin the forest, hever.'

'The weather was always warm,' continued Zoe. 'It never rained, and school didn't exist.' She paused. 'Halfway through the film a scream of anguish came from the row where you were sitting. The movie stopped and all the lights went on. "Take me ome," you told your grandmother in a heartbroken voice. "Hi cannert bear it hany lernger." What couldn't you bear exactly?' Zoe asked.

'The beauty erf the world I saw hin the movie,' he explained. 'I erlready knew that life was nert like that. Did they sink they cerd furl me with a lie?'

Zoe patted his hands. 'But your grandmother claims

your childhood wasn't as miserable as you say. Some nice things must have happened,' she coaxed.

'When I turned nine,' the Frog shrugged, 'my merther came frem Paris and terk me to a restaurant fur my berthday. I hordered coq au vin, bert hit wers badly cerked, so I sent hit berk to the kitchen. The chef came hout and said Monsieur sherd learn to heat wert e wers given. I terld him e wers han himbecile. I said e sherd ave glazed the honions hin sugar and red wine, and that e ad been far too heconomicerl avec the wine hin the dish.'

Howard pulled a pen from his pocket and began making notes—on glazing onions in sugar and red wine—on the back of his hand.

'I asked the chef hif e wers French, er han himmigrant. E grabbed my merther's wine and purred it hin my meal.'

'So he was French after all,' remarked Howard. 'Tell me, was it that experience which predisposed you to not liking restaurants in general?'

'Mais non,' the Frog replied. 'I dern't like restaurants becurse I nevaire ave room to move. The chairs and tables are erlways too smerll. I ham erlways serffercating, and you're nert herllowed to smoke.'

'You went away to boarding school at the age of ten,' continued Zoe, returning to the letter. 'But you never stopped complaining about the food, and in the end they expelled you for constantly demanding grilled pigs' trotters for dinner. You were sent to other schools, and were expelled from them as well.'

'Bouf! They cerd nert teach me hanysing.'

'At fourteen, during a summer holiday at Belle-Ile, you began an affair with the twenty-three-year-old daughter of some family friends.'

'I longed for vacations like that too,' sighed Howard.

'It hended badly,' the Frog told him. 'The first time Simone cerked me dinner, she burnt the flageolet beans—and erl my life, I keep meeting wormen who can't cerk.'

'Thanks,' said Zoe. 'I'll remember that.'

Howard glanced at his watch. 'Is that the time? I'm meant to be dropping Antarctica off at her psychoanalyst's. I have to go.'

'Can't you make a quick prognosis first?' Zoe asked.

'Well,' said Howard, turning to the Frog, 'in brief, when you see food, your emotional controls shut down, while at the same time your sensory data reveals a personal reality that veers recklessly towards a free association with cholesterol. This isn't too big a problem in itself, but your responses reveal false positive-negative signals that seemed to be rooted in a disorientation of self.'

'He means you're a glutton,' Zoe translated.

'No,' the psychiatrist rebuked her, 'it means—well—look, I'd like to write the Frog up as a case history, as long as he has no objections.'

'Mais non!' the Frog told him grandly. 'Herf curse you merst write me herp. This is pert erf my durstiny!'

'Have you thought about taking anti-depressants?' Howard asked, as Zoe and the Frog walked him to the door. 'They might help you to see things more in perspective.'

'I see sings hin perspective now,' the Frog replied. 'Herther people get depressed hin middle age, becurse they realise they will nevaire ave the sert herf life they wernted. I knew I werd nevaire ave the sert erf life I wernted when I wers five. I nevaire lived hin the paradise erf the furl.'

'Well, what's your answer then?' said Howard, a bit niggly about this reversal in roles. He was one of Sydney's top psychiatrists—not the Frog.

'Zoe and I merst go to France,' shouted the Frog, out of the blue. 'It his himperative we leave himmediately! Termerrow! My grandmerther's letter as made me omeseek fur my cerntry, heven though I ham still herpset about the frozen cassoulet. I ave the keys to han hempty hapartment hin Paris belernging to a friend who lives hin Guadeloupe. E went there hinstead erf me. I will nevaire furgive im. E as a guilty conscience, so we can stay hin is hapartment has lerng has we like. I will berk the plane tickets right haway.'

'This is crazy. I can't afford to fly to France right now,' Zoe protested, even though she was already imagining afternoons strolling through the Tuileries, dreaming of the ghosts of literary figures past. 'Anyway, it costs a fortune to fly from Australia to France if you don't book months ahead.'

'There's no time to berk mernths ahead. I nevaire berk mernths ahead! I ham himperlsive! I do sings by hinstinct. Dern't werry about the cerst—I ave a leetle hegg nest hin France fur my rainy day. You can pay me berk later ern.'

He rushed off to fetch the telephone book.

'Zoe, you *must* go with him,' Howard urged. 'Don't you see? It's the perfect opportunity to observe the Frog in his natural habitat rather than misplaced in an Anglo-Saxon setting. Think of the ground-breaking paper I could write on the results of living out of context, based on your observations.'

'Then study me,' Zoe suggested. 'God knows, *I* live out of context.'

Howard waved her egocentricism aside. 'Please, Zoe, think of my reputation.'

'You expect me to play research assistant for you, when I'm trying to write a novel about how someone is murdering all the Booker Prize judges?'

'I thought,' Howard said, surprised, 'your novel didn't have a plot.'

'I changed my mind,' said Zoe. 'I'm combining it with my original idea of exploring the banality of the real—or the unreal, I haven't made up my mind which, yet. So the last thing I feel like doing is accompanying a camembert-eating lunatic back to his original environment.'

'I ham nert a lernatic,' said the Frog, reappearing in the hall. 'I ham a relic left-hover frem a civilisation the world furgot. Wern day, the gods will cerm berk and claim me.'

'You see?' Howard said to Zoe. 'Another insight!'

'Dern't werry about a visa, Zoe,' the Frog interrupted him. 'I'll jerst say you and I are married.'

'I have an EC passport, thank you. I'm a New Zealander, but my father's English,' Zoe answered.

'The gynaecologist! I merst cernserlt im the moment e returns,' the Frog remembered. 'Whenhever I heat, my stermach swells erp. This his nert nermel!'

'How long do you think you'll be gone?' Howard asked, steering the conversation back to Paris. 'You did promise to have a dinner party and I've been looking forward to it. Can we ave coq au vin again?'

'Herf curse we can. Dern't werry. We'll be berk befur you know hit.'

These words struck Zoe as strangely prophetic, although she couldn't work out why. 'You won't be able to get seats on a plane at this late stage,' she said instead.

'Why nert?' the Frog argued. 'Dern't be negative. Au

revoir, Howard. I merst phern the hairline himmediately!'

'Wait!' said Howard. 'One other thing. What happened to the baby-teeth your grandmother enclosed with her letter?'

'I pert them hin the scarecrow hin the garden,' the Frog replied. He was already dialling the number of the airline, like a man possessed.

'This trip is going to be a nightmare—I just know it,' said Zoe in a low voice, opening the front door and walking with Howard out onto the landing.

'Courage, Zoe. Close your eyes and think of Notre Dame.'

Zoe returned to the living room to find the Frog shouting down the phone. 'I'm terking to a bluddy machine!' he spluttered. 'I cannert get through. They wernt to pert me hin a queue! Houtrageous!' He slammed down the phone and lit a cigarette. 'I ave to go to Paris! His that too merch to hask? I dern't know ow lerng I ave left to me hin this life!'

'Oh, not that old line again,' Zoe sighed. 'Look, why don't we just eat the foie gras and go to Paris some other time?'

The Frog dialled the airline again, and Zoe, with a resigned expression on her face, went to her room to start packing. Just in case. She was putting her laptop in a bag when she heard him spluttering.

'Allo? I ave been waiting hin this bluddy queue fur weeks! Perdern? I wernt two seats avec lerts erf leg room. I ave very lerng legs and I can nevaire fit them hin your planes. Merde! Non, I wersn't speaking to you—I'm trying to hopen a berttle erf sauterne. Can I horder my meal now? Why nert? Are you BYO yet?'

Zoe got out her passport. She heard the Frog making another call. This time he spoke in rapid French. 'Oui, oh oui!' he shouted at one stage, causing her to hurry into the living room. Was he having phone sex with Monique?

'Who were you ringing?' she demanded, as he hung up.

'I ave horganised a leetle celebration fur you hin Paris. You will like it very merch,' the Frog replied mysteriously, handing her a glass of sauterne. 'It's very himpertant fur hour relationship.'

'We don't have a relationship, remember?'

'Bert Zoe, you are cerming to Paris with me!'

'As far as I'm concerned,' said Zoe, 'I'm accompanying you to Paris to gain more inspiration for my novel. Don't even think about taking me for a moonlight stroll along the Seine, or whispering the recipe for sauteed eels in my ear. It's not going to work. Got it?'

'Hokay,' said the Frog. He started sniggering quietly to himself, much to Zoe's irritation. 'I'm going to go and perk,' he said, walking into the kitchen.

'What do you need from there? Your vegetable peelers?' Zoe inquired with heavy sarcasm from the doorway.

'Non, the foie gras, so we dern't sterve ern the plane.'

'You can't take foie gras on board!'

'Why nert?' he countered, walking past her with the foie gras, a can opener, a knife and a packet of mini-toast. 'I erlways take my hown food ern the plane. It's erful to harrive ern Paris ern han hempty stermach.'

'It might help you to occasionally go hungry,' Zoe called after him. 'When Hemingway wrote about Paris in *A Moveable Feast*, he said that the paintings in the Luxembourg Museum were all the more beautiful on an empty belly, and that he learned to understand Cézanne much better and to see truly how he made his landscapes. He even wondered if Cézanne painted when he was hungry.'

'Emingway wers serch han hidiot,' the Frog shouted back, walking down the hall towards his bedroom.

Zoe stared moodily at the Brassai photograph in the living room of the elderly men in the cafe drinking wine. The Frog had said that he would end up like them, and sometimes she sensed there was another existence waiting for her as well. That was what she meant when she told Howard she was living out of context. At times she even glimpsed this other life; she saw trees shimmering in summer heat, a book left lying on a tennis court, the tiled rooftops of an ancient city, a dish of green papaya. Perhaps it was the fate of all writers to confuse memory with imagination. She wished there was someone literary with whom she could discuss this living-out-of-context business. Imagine, for instance, living in the same neighbourhood as Elias Canetti, and having coffee with him every afternoon.

Zoe was a great fan of Canetti. One of her best-loved books was *The Secret Heart of the Clock*. 'What was it about life—which you have known after all—that aroused your enthusiasm? Its persistence in memory,' were the first lines of Canetti she had ever read.

'Merde!' came a scream. 'Ow am I meant to fit the foie gras *and* my terthbresh hin my toilert berg? Why sherd I ave to cherse?'

Zoe took *The Secret Heart of the Clock* from one of the bookshelves she had annexed and returned to her room.

'Why do I ave to be persecuted by my lerggerge? I ate my sertcase! I ate carrying sings! I wernt ter be has free has a berd!'

Letting the book fall open, her eyes fell on the following lines. 'It would be beautiful to disappear. Nowhere to be found. It would be beautiful to be the only one to know that you have disappeared.'

She thought some more about these lines and realised, in one of those rare moments of crystalline thought, that in writing and rewriting her novel, deleting line after line, the original novel had, effectively, disappeared. Unfortunately, she had no idea how to restore the words she had abandoned. But was that the point? Her novel, in its original form, was too pure to be published. Ah, of course—that was it. The vanished words would remain forever her secret. They had to in any case, since she could no longer remember what she had written.

'Are you ill?'

The question came from a customs officer with the sharp eyes of someone trained to notice anything amiss, and who had been watching the Frog with increasing concern as he tottered towards passport control.

'Herf curse I ham hill!' moaned the wild-eyed passenger. 'I ham sinking habout being trapped hin a sardine can fur the next twenty-four hours!'

Zoe, already through passport control, turned around, exasperated. Now they'd probably want to search him, and find the foie gras hidden in the toilet bag in his carry-on luggage—which they might just put down to French elitism, except he had camembert in there as well, which was pushing his luck. The mystery was that the can opener hadn't set off the X-ray machine. Could a can opener be defined as an illegal weapon?

'Please take no notice. He always exaggerates,' she said to the passport officer. 'He thinks the airline shrinks the seats each year to get more passengers on.'

'And why do I ave to wear a seatbolt?' the Frog demanded. 'I ham nert going to furll hout erf the plane, ham I?'

The officer, who looked the type who spent his weekends on clifftops with binoculars, searching the horizon for boatloads of illegal immigrants, took the Frog's passport and studied it with an expression that did not augur well.

'Now you ave to stamp my pisspot so that heverywern knows I ham leaving the cerntry. Will hit nevaire hend?'

There was something else the passport officer excelled at, and that was belligerence. This quality always came to the fore when challenged by a member of the public with a foreign accent. 'I'm getting pretty sick and tired of dealing with people like you,' he said. 'If you don't like things the way they are, why don't you go back to your own country and stay there? And you'd better get a move on, because the final boarding call for your flight was almost ten minutes ago.'

'It's nert hour ferlt!' argued the Frog. 'There were too many jellyfish ern the road!'

The officer's expression hardened further and he put a restraining hand on the Frog's arm. 'Have you been taking drugs, sir?'

The introduction of 'sir' in the dialogue suggested serious trouble.

'No, truly, he hasn't,' Zoe said hastily. 'He's referring to the traffic. You know how horrible the French can be about other motorists.'

'You wernt ter sniff me avec your dergs?' the Frog went on, his voice rising. 'Wert do you sink they're going to find? A garlic hin my hanus?'

'Shut up,' Zoe hissed, 'or they'll confiscate the foie gras.'

'Anyway, your dergs are a waste erf time,' barked the Frog. 'Why dern't you train them to sniff hout trerffles hinstead?'

'I'm so sorry,' Zoe interrupted. 'He's a little agitated about the flight. That's probably why he had leek soup for breakfast, followed by a stale creme caramel.'

The danger escalated. 'I think I've heard about you,' the officer said, 'from my brother.'

'It's quite perssiberl. Many fureigners nertice me,' the Frog said grandly. 'I ham nert heasy to furget.'

'My brother is a parking warden,' the officer went on. 'Do you remember now?'

'I dern't sink I know hany perking wardens,' the Frog

replied, shuddering in an exaggerated manner. 'Ernless I ave trerdden ern wern with my fert, mistaking im fur a cerkroach. Per'aps that's why my fert got gout two days ago.'

'Open your bag, sir.'

'Why? Nowern helse ad to hopen their bergs! Are you trying to hannoy me ern purpose?'

'Just open it, before I call security.'

'Oh no,' Zoe moaned. 'We'll miss the plane.'

The officer began rummaging around in the Frog's bag in a manner which clearly indicated the Frog was for the high jump. 'People like you,' he said, taking out a bottle of olive oil, a can of goose fat, Dijon mustard, a machine for blending parsley and garlic, some wine vinegar, a jar of gherkins and a quail leg, 'have no idea how to behave in a civilised country, do you? Why don't you take a goat on board as well?'

'I dern't ave a goat,' replied the Frog, 'bert sank you fur suggesting it. I erlways wernted to ave a goat, with a leetle bell haround is neck, hand a ferm-ouse hin the Pyrenees.'

The passport officer thumped the table with his fist. 'What are you doing with all this food?' he shouted.

'I erlways take food ern berd!' the Frog shouted back. 'Wert appens if we crash hin the jerngerl? Ow are we going to survive?'

The officer reached for his walkie-talkie. Zoe, whose

first concern was still the toilet bag, grabbed the walkie-talkie and held it behind her back. 'His psychiatrist says it's okay for him to travel—honestly,' she pleaded.

The PA burst into life. 'WOULD THE FOLLOWING TWO PASSENGERS MAKE THEIR WAY TO DEPARTURE LOUNGE TWELVE IMMEDIATELY!' ordered an annoyed female voice. 'THE PASSENGERS ARE...'

'That's us!' cried Zoe. 'We'll have to run! Why don't you keep the quail leg?' she suggested to the official. 'Think of it as a gift.'

'Non!' shrieked the Frog. 'It's mine. E's nert serperssed to haccept bribes!'

The passport official held onto the quail leg, and smiled evilly at the Frog. 'You'd better get out of here,' he said.

'Why dern't you take the Dijon mersterd too?' snarled the Frog, thrusting it at him. 'It's bettaire with the quail. Do I ave to tell you heverysing?'

Zoe threw everything else back in the bag and grabbed his arm. 'Come on! We're going to miss the plane.'

Dragging him by the arm, she and the Frog reached the departure lounge where one of the ground staff was waiting. 'You're very late!' she snapped. 'They almost left without you!'

'The pisspot man sterl my quail leg, *hand* the Dijon mersterd,' roared the Frog. 'Hit's han houtrage.'

'There's plenty of food on the plane,' the woman replied. 'Nobody starves on any of our flights.'

'I erlways sterve ern your flights!' the Frog contradicted her. 'I ave been sterving erl erf my life! That's why we're going back to Paris. I ham taking Zoe to—' He suddenly broke off. 'We are ready to go ern berd, now,' he said imperiously, as if it was all his own idea. 'Please show us to hour seats.'

The plane was full. As it taxied down the runway, Zoe let out a long sigh of relief. 'What were you about to say back then?' she asked, once they were airborne.

'I furgert,' replied the Frog. He looked irritably around at their fellow passengers. 'Lerk at erl those vegetaberls, sitting hin their leetle rows. Wert orriberl specimens erf umanity.' He started fidgeting in his seat. 'I'm serffurcating. I cannert breeze. Why are the seats erlways so smerll? My leg his getting a crermp.'

Zoe, gazing out the window, ignored him. The plane climbed towards a vast bank of clouds. She thought about the message she'd left on Ian's answering machine explaining that their lunch would have to be postponed because she'd had to go to Paris, in the way that serious writers often did. She didn't mention the exciting, new direction the novel had veered off in—which was just as well, she realised, because perhaps it wasn't such a good idea to have someone killing all the judges of the Booker Prize. She didn't want the judges to get the wrong idea and discriminate against her.

'I ope the pilert knows wert e's doing. I sink we're flying hin the wrerng direction.'

Zoe pushed the Booker judges from her mind. 'I still haven't worked out where you put the can opener,' she said, trying to distract the Frog before he could start causing more chaos. 'It can't be in your toilet bag, otherwise it would have set off the alarm.'

'Hit his hin my toilet berg,' boasted the Frog. 'I rerbbed hit with garlic—hit erlways werks. Shall we heat the foie gras now?'

'Why don't we keep it until later?' she suggested. 'I'm going to work on my novel. There's a major element I have to change. Why don't you have a siesta until lunch?'

'I cannert ave a siesta. My cremp his getting werse.' The Frog started twisting and turning in his seat. 'I sink I ham aving han hemergency,' he announced.

A blue-eyed flight attendant with Beatrice Dalle lips, her hair pulled back into a chignon, paused as she was passing.

'His hanysing wreng?' she asked.

'Oh God! Not another one,' Zoe thought. 'I should write a protest letter to the French government about the way their nationals keep popping up.'

The Frog and the French hostess, after beaming at one another, swapped information about where they were born, where they grew up, and briefly discussed how mighty sure of themselves New Zealand and Australian wine-growers were getting of late. Then they turned their attention to the pressing matter of the Frog's leg. 'It's too lerng fur the seat,' the Frog explained. 'I tried to tell the woman hat the hairline desk that my legs nevaire fit hin the plane, bert she said she eard that frogs' legs were smerll henerf to fit hin han haverage-sized dinner plate.'

'Wert Hanglo-Saxon nerve!' exclaimed the flight attendant. 'Ow dare she hinserlt you like that!'

'Hexactly ow I felt,' nodded the Frog. 'Bert since she *did* mention frogs' legs, I sert I werd tell er ow to cerk them—hin buttaire and garlic, with serm parsley, served ern a bed erf rice. She hactually asked me ow lerng she sherd cerk them!'

'Hanglo-Saxons!' said the hostess, shaking her head.

'I know! So I terld er, "huntil they are cerked, herf curse!" Bert I dern't sink she wers listening. And now I ham hin hagony.' He went on, 'I ope my leg dersn't ave to be hamputated, like my fert erlmost wers the erther day. His there a surgeon ern berd?'

'I dern't sink so,' the flight attendant replied, looking concerned. 'Can you try to sternd herp? It might jerst need serm hexercise.'

'I cannert spend the hentire flight hexercising my leg,'

the Frog pointed out. 'Bert you cerd erlways tell the pilert I need hanerther seat.'

'I'll do hit straight away,' his countrywoman promised. 'You're right. These seats are scanderlersly smerll.' She hurried back up the aisle in the direction of the cockpit.

The Frog turned to Zoe, who had her laptop open on her tray-table, and was ostentatiously staring at the screen. 'My stermach his a mess,' he whined. 'It's erl the tension erf aving to rersh to catch the plane. I need to go to the berthroom.'

'Good idea,' said Zoe. 'That will give you something to do until Mademoiselle comes back with a new seating plan.' She didn't look up as the Frog got out his toilet bag and left.

Fifteen minutes later he was back. 'This plane his a dersgrace!' he said furiously. 'I demand han hexplernation!'

A steward, who was strolling the aisles chatting to the passengers, rushed over. 'Is anything the matter?' he asked.

'The toilet his too smerll!' the Frog shouted. 'I can nevaire fit hin! Who do you're sink I ham—Toulouse-Lautrec?'

The steward cleared his throat, bemused. 'The toilets are standard size, sir,' he said. 'And Mr Lertrack, whoever he is, hasn't made any complaints.' He flashed a professional smile—he had fabulous teeth—and continued on his public relations circuit.

The French flight attendant, her face flushed, re-appeared, wringing her hands. 'I ham so serry,' she said, 'bert the pilert said the plane his furl, and you will jerst ave to try and cope. I cerd serve you dinner, hif you like, befur hanywern helse. We ave poulet, feesh, er veal.'

'Bert I wernted serm seared schnapper hin a garlic and mersterd seed crerst,' the Frog whimpered. 'I cannert sterp sinking habout the schnapper I missed hat Ziggi's.'

The hostess looked sweetly sympathetic. 'You had bettaire ave the feesh.'

'Is that hit?' the Frog asked indignantly, a short time later. 'Bert there's nussing there!'

'You cerd ave serm mere cashew nerts, hif you like,' the flight attendant suggested in desperation.

'I ham nert a chipmernk,' the Frog chided her.

A second, more senior, flight attendant, who had been advancing up the aisle with the dinner trolley, stopped next to her colleague. Suntanned, fit, wearing a little too much make-up, she gave the Frog the kind of fresh, sunny smile that comes from years of intense sexual experience. 'You're French, aren't you?' she said. 'Sophie, was telling me about you just before. I'll take over now,' she said to Sophie. 'You're needed up the front. I'm Trish,' she continued, staring directly at the Frog. 'Ouch! My G-string is rubbing against my sunburn. I should have used more blockout on my bum. Or *berm*, as you French say. Your accent is really sexy,' she went on. 'It's got that ge ne says quat about it.'

'Oh, sank you,' the Frog simpered. 'Ow nice you are. Husually, with Hanglo-Saxons, I ave to struggerl to be hundersterd.'

'I'd like to see you struggle,' said Trish, changing her stance so that the Frog was now gazing directly at her groin.

'Perhaps you shouldn't mention your feelings about Anglo-Saxon pubic hair at this point,' Zoe mumbled, from her seat next to the window, 'although I imagine Trish shaves hers off.'

The passenger sitting behind the Frog, a public servant type with a huffy way of speaking, leaned forward and tapped her on the arm. 'Unfortunately, I don't have a French accent, but I would like some dinner,' he said.

'Ferkwerd,' mumbled the Frog, as Trish handed the other passenger a meal without bothering to look at him. He then caressed Trish's elbow. 'I ham serch a glurton,' he chuckled. 'That is why I need mere dinner. I will tell you a leetle secret. Today, hit's my berthday—so this his my leetle berthday dinner.'

'It is *not* your birthday,' Zoe broke in. 'Your birthday was three days ago.'

'Bouf!' said the Frog. 'Hit seems like yesterday. And you premised you were going to terk me hout fur dinner.' He turned to Trish with a sorrowful expression. 'She didn't.'

'Well, that wasn't very nice, was it?' said Trish. She bent down and whispered in the Frog's ear, 'I'll tell you what—First Class is having plums in brandy. I'll bring you one later on for dessert.'

'I'll have one too, thanks,' said Zoe, who had excellent hearing.

Trish pursed her lips and straightened up. 'I can probably only spare one,' she said. She pushed the trolley further up the aisle and served the other passengers.

Half an hour later she was back, with one serving of plums in brandy. 'Sorry,' she said to Zoe, 'but he asked first.' She let her hip brush against the Frog. 'Are you happy now?' she asked him.

'Don't answer that question, please,' Zoe ordered him. 'You don't want to destroy Trish's uncomplicated view of life.' But there was no stopping him.

'Wert his appiness?' wondered the Frog. 'I ave nevaire known the answer to that question. Erl my life, hit as managed to helude me. I first noticed this when I wers ern my perty, and no wern came to perll me erf. I realised then that life wers going to be wern uge struggerl, and I ave nert been proved wreng yet. I ham doomed. There his no ope.'

'You really need to update that line,' said Zoe. 'And you've upset Trish.' Trish pulled a face then moved off quickly down the aisle without a backward glance.

The Frog ate his plums in brandy without offering Zoe a taste. 'Hit's very smerll,' he sighed. 'I can nevaire ave wert I wernt.'

'Cheer up. We've still got our secret stash of pate de foie gras,' Zoe reminded him.

The Frog looked stricken and developed a violent itch on one of his shoulder blades. 'I don't sink I ave the foie gras hanymere,' he said, going into contortions as he tried to get a hand up to the spot. 'Can you scratch my berk please, Zoe?'

'What are you talking about?' Zoe demanded, and she didn't mean his itch. 'It's in your toilet bag. You said so before.'

'I merst ave left hit behind,' the Frog said desperately. 'Hor helse, the pisspot hofficial sterl hit. Erl I know, is that hit's no lernger hanywhere to be ferned.'

'You ate it, didn't you! When you went off to the toilet and stayed there for so long.'

'I cerd nert elp hit!' argued the Frog. 'I wers werried the cabin pressure werd make hit go erf.'

'Did you eat all of it?'

'The cans are very smerll. It's nert my ferlt! I hate hit by mistake!'

Zoe stared at him, her lips set in a grim line. 'I don't want to speak to you for the rest of the trip,' she said finally. 'Your greed is absolutely unbelievable.'

'Why are you being so nersty?' asked the Frog. Zoe changed her position as much as possible in the restricted space, so that he ended up staring at the back of her head. 'Hokay,' he said, when there was no answer, 'if you wern't terk to me, I ham going to knerck myself erp.'

'Please do,' she encouraged him, watching from out of the corner of her eye as the Frog made a great display of opening a packet of sleeping pills.

'You asked fur this,' the Frog said haughtily. Zoe made no reply. 'And dern't try to woke me!'

She started writing. She had got eleven words down when the Frog's head slumped onto his chest and he started snoring. He was a five-star snorer, Zoe realised. His snores resounded throughout the plane to the point where other passengers started complaining.

'I'm so sorry,' Zoe replied each time. 'I only met him on the plane. I'm afraid he's not my responsibility.'

She wrote on, following yet another new literary trail, oblivious to the countries passing below. She gradually drifted into a state of nothingness where she wasn't sure whether she was writing, or dreaming that she was. Writing was often like this for her. Somewhere over the Black Forest, her eyes closed.

The Frog shook her awake. 'Zoe, we're landing in

alf an hour. I brershed my teeth and wershed my face and pert serm perfume ern.'

Zoe decided not to ask whose toothbrush he had used. She already knew the answer. 'You owe me some foie gras,' she said.

'Bert herf curse!' cried the revitalised Frog, pulling out a dozen or so miniature French flags, and handing them out to the nearest passengers.

'What are we meant to do with these?' one passenger asked.

'You wave it has you dishemberk,' beamed the Frog. 'Then they know you are friendly and they will treat you has wern erf ers.'

Just before 4 p.m. they touched down at Charles de Gaulle Airport. The sky was a bleached-out pale blue, although that could change, the Frog warned Zoe, as they left the plane. 'It's the beginning erf spring hin Paris. You nevaire know wert the weather will do.'

Passing through French customs with a Frenchman was, Zoe realised sourly, a very different matter from arriving in Paris on her own. 'Bouf!' said the first official, when she handed him her passport. 'Bouf!' they said at customs. Only one uniformed figure asked offhandedly, 'Anysing to decler?' And when Zoe answered, 'Him', indicating the Frog, the man replied coldly, 'Madame, dern't be sew hinserlting.'

There was a long queue for taxis outside. Just as the Frog had warned, the weather was changing. A long band of clouds had begun moving in, and there was a feeling of rain in the air. The English, Dutch, German, Chinese, Japanese, Swiss and Swedish travellers stood waiting patiently, shivering a little after the warmth inside the terminal. The French, on the other hand, worked themselves into a state of apoplexy within minutes of joining the queue. One man, in a crumpled suit, his coat folded over his arm, hurled his briefcase into the road in frustration.

'What's his problem?' Zoe asked. 'There's a whole line of taxis approaching.'

Instantly, all the French within earshot, including the Frog, shouted in unison, 'That his nert the point!' The Frog explained further, 'Why sherd we be furced to wait hat erl?'

Their own taxi, when it arrived, reeked of garlic and pork sausage. Despite the lateness of the hour, the driver, a large, pasty-faced man wearing a thick brown jacket, had evidently only just finished lunch. 'Madame as been here befur?' he asked, ramming his foot down on the accelerator. Zoe didn't bother answering. She couldn't bear the smell in the car, and besides, the driver was too busy honking his horn and overtaking every other motorist on the road. He didn't address her again until they had entered the centre of Paris. As the car skidded around a corner, narrowly missing a poodle which had raced away from its owner, he said, 'Paris as changed fur the werst. Too many fureigners,' he added unpleasantly, braking as they almost ploughed into a snarl of traffic.

'Do you mind telling him I'm not interested in his racist remarks?' Zoe said to the Frog. 'I'm trying to experience Paris as a writer profoundly affected by the sight of white shutters behind black wrought-iron balconies.'

The Frog wasn't listening. He was gazing out the window, in raptures at the sight of so many Parisians in the streets depite the sprinkling rain.

'Lerk at that! Honly the French know the art erf leaving!' he shouted, tears of pride pouring down his face as the taxi passed a semi-naked couple making love with abandon on the bonnet of a Citroen.

'I think you mean living,' said Zoe.

He ignored her. 'The Hanglo-Saxons werd sit hinside and ave a cerp erf tea!' he roared, as they came to another halt, this time outside a pavement cafe packed with Parisians getting plastered. 'Merci! Merci!' he blubbered, as the owner of the cafe handed him a glass of Pernod through the taxi window.

A moment later they passed a man in workman's clothes who was leaning against a van, sipping a glass of claret and exchanging loud insults about the European Union with his workmates. 'Bravo!' screamed the Frog. 'Long leave France!'

A third halt in the traffic prompted the taxi driver to throw the Gauloise he was smoking out the window in disgust. 'Putain de traffic!' he exploded, giving the finger to the cars in front, whose owners were doing the same to everyone else, and so on right along the rue.

'Oh look! There's Gerard Depardieu!' cried Zoe above the din. An overweight man with long straggly hair walked past the taxi, wiping his nose with a finger. 'No, no, there's Gerard Depardieu!' she corrected herself, as a blond, skinny man in a tight leather jacket, crossed the road eating a baguette from a bag. 'What could I have been thinking? *There's* Gerard Depardieu,' she breathed in awe. An unshaven lout, with a cigarette dangling from his lip, started peeing up against a metro entrance.

'Hokay, Zoe, I sink I eard henerf,' the Frog said crossly.

The cars jolted back into life. Soon after, the taxi pulled up outside a building with intricate stonework over the entrance, and dormer windows in the roof, at the side of a small square lined with chestnut trees.

Zoe was more than pleasantly surprised. She had expected some sort of pseudo-bohemian slum whose entrance was through the side door of a charcuterie. She stood on the pavement while the driver grudgingly opened the boot to get the luggage. She imagined she was a Parisian, a resident of the building. She could see herself crossing the square each morning to have coffee at the cafe on the corner, before setting down to work on her latest Prix Goncourt. A new plot was beginning to suggest itself. A woman writer, living out of context, travels to Paris to explore her literary relationship with the ghost of Proust, meets the head of the Russian Mafia who is in Paris doing business with a French oil company, falls in love with him (he is a Bulgakov fan as well), witnesses his assassination and flees to a Greek island to write the book about what happens...Then what? Zoe sighed. That's why plots were such literary let-downs. You had to have a beginning, a middle and an end. You couldn't wander freely, without structure, exploring the writer within.

'Are you going to stand ern the pavement erl hevening?' the Frog demanded. 'I wernt to hopen serm champagne himmediately to celebrate hour harriverl.'

The apartment, belonging to his friend in Guadeloupe, was just like the Frog's flat in Sydney, on the second floor. It had a bedroom with heavy furniture which looked Spanish, a bathroom with a great number of silver taps, a living room with paintings of old steamships covering every wall and a loft with a Caribbean-style mosquito net concealing a double mattress on the floor.

'It's a nice mosquito net, hisn't it?' the Frog said to Zoe. 'There are lerts erf mosquitoes hin Paris at this time erf year. I sink we had bettaire sleep hin the lerft to be ern the safe side.'

'Nice try,' Zoe answered. 'You can take the loft. I'll sleep in the bedroom.'

'Hokay, Zoe,' sighed the Frog. 'I will jerst ave to haccept that you are hexploiting me.'

'What do you mean?' Zoe demanded.

'I ham taking you to wern erf the merst glamorous places hin Paris tonight and you still hinsist ern playing ard to get.'

'Is it far from here?' Zoe asked, mentally running through some possibilities. Drinks at the Elysee Palace? A glittering nightclub somewhere off the Champs Elysees? Dinner at Francoise Sagan's house?

'It's about twernty minutes werk away,' the Frog replied. 'Hernless you feel too tired. We cerd take hanerther taxi.'

'No thanks,' said Zoe quickly. 'I'd rather walk. I always walk in Paris. I could walk around Paris all day and all night.'

'I cerdn't,' the Frog grumbled. 'I still ave a ser fert, remember?'

'I suppose so,' said Zoe, not taking much notice of him. She went off to take a shower.

'Will this do?' she said when she appeared in the living room again. She had on her Mario Vargas Llosa-induced black catsuit—well, she reasoned, they might very well run into him in Paris—over which was a mock leopard-skin jacket she had bought during another visit to Paris, years earlier. She had justified the expense at the time by concluding that the odds that she might run into Bernard-Henri Levy in some narrow rue on the Left Bank were probably quite high.

The Frog, who was waiting for her with two glasses of excellent champagne and some foie gras he had found in a cupboard, was overcome. 'Zoe! I lerve this jacket! I ham going to dress erp too!'

'Oh yes?' said Zoe, in a disbelieving tone. Then she imagined Howard frowning at her, and clinked her champagne glass with the Frog's.

'Why don't you dress like that all the time?' she asked with pleasure, when he finally made his entrance. For a moment, she had thought the absent owner of the apartment had just arrived. The Frog was wearing a black cashmere jacket over a pair of elegant trousers, and his aviator's scarf draped gracefully around his neck. She was amazed.

They left the apartment and went down into the street. Zoe, affected by champagne, jet lag and Parisian emotion, found herself stealing looks at the Frog. His profile seemed unusually noble when set against the lyrical extravagance of the well-lit art nouveau buildings they were passing, and his unstyled, untidy hair, she could now see, suited the setting perfectly. Swirling romantically around his head, his hair could have been designed by Jules Lavirotte himself. He looked so different from the man she had met in Sydney. He looked *in context,* she realised with a pang. 'You must have used that expensive French shampoo in the shower,' she commented. 'Your hair looks so nice and full.'

'Oui, furll has the hauterm leaves befur they ferll,' sighed the Frog, lighting a cigarette.

Oh well, thought Zoe, some things never change. She briefly wondered about the curious scuffling sound she kept hearing.

They crossed a boulevard and entered a different neighbourhood, one that wasn't quite as stylish. The art nouveau architecture had started to thin out, and the streets had become more nondescript. They came to an anonymous little rue with nothing to distinguish it, save for a shop selling old prints and maps, which was closed.

'Ere we are!' announced the Frog, clasping his hands in delight. 'Wersn't that worse the wait?'

Puzzled, Zoe glanced around her. People were queuing up outside a small cinema on the corner, opposite a restaurant with the name, 'Pierre's Le Pied de Cochon' printed in peeling letters above the door. 'Where?' she asked.

'There!' the Frog cried with delirious excitement, gesturing towards the restaurant. 'I cerd ardly wait to bring you ere! They serve the best pigs' trertters hin Paris!'

Zoe felt as if someone had thumped her in the kidneys, then injected paralysing fluid into her veins. She couldn't move a muscle, and she was having trouble breathing.

The Frog, uncomprehending, took her by the arm. 'Hisn't it wernderferl? Why dern't you say hanysing, Zoe? Dern't you lerve my surprise?' His eyes were fixed on the words over the restaurant door. 'Wert's the matter, Zoe? Why are you dragging your feets?'

'It's some kind of trick, isn't it?' Zoe whispered. 'You want me to think you brought me all the way to Paris to eat the feet of murdered pigs. Very funny. You wore a black cashmere jacket and began to look like a real Frenchman, to come to a place where they specialise in pigs' trotters. Can we go to Francoise Sagan's now?'

But the Frog was coaxing her towards the restaurant. The owner was standing on the doorstep, waiting to greet them. Disguising a belch behind his hand, he waved them into his abattoir—a medium-sized room with sixteen tables, nearly all of which were full. The furnishings were old-fashioned: bentwood chairs, flocked wallpaper and lampshades with brown tassels. Paintings of pastoral scenes hung above the till.

'You merst be Hinglish, madame,' he said politely, when Zoe failed to respond to his greeting. 'Cerngratulations. Ere, you will heat real food at lerst!' Pulling out her chair with an exaggerated gesture, the owner signalled for some menus before going off to attend to some other customers.

Zoe sat down and stared vacantly ahead. Her catsuit, her mock leopard-skin jacket, coming to Paris—what had been the point? Suddenly she lost all restraint. 'Why did you bring me to this awful place?' she yelled at the Frog, picking up the salt and throwing it at him.

The hum in the restaurant stopped as the other diners put down their knives and forks, and stared. 'That's the prerblem with France these days!' commented the Frog, brushing salt off his jacket. 'Heverywern speaks Hinglish. Sermsing merst be dern befur the French language becerms hextinct.'

The owner, shocked by Zoe's behaviour, hurried over. 'Hour pigs' trertters are the best hin France, I premise you, madame,' he stammered, looking distressed. 'Bert we can cerk them serm kind erf Hinglish way hif you wernt.'

'I don't want them at all, as a matter of fact,' Zoe snapped. 'Do you have some celery sticks and aioli, or a salad nicoise?'

'Oh, Zoe!' said the Frog. 'Why are you sew difficerlt?'

'I'm not difficult,' Zoe replied. 'Other people are difficult. I'm calm, until other people upset me.'

'Bert Zoe, this is wern erf my favourite restaurants hin Paris!' He looked so mournful that Zoe began to feel defeated. Why did the French have to be so tragic about food?

'I thought you hated restaurants,' she said wearily.

'Nert erl erf them,' replied the Frog, still speaking more in sorrow than in anger. 'I lerve serm erf them very merch. Hespecially in France, where you're still allowed to smerk.'

'We dern't ave any celery sticks, madame,' the patron miserably interrupted. 'I jerst cernserlted the chef. E said e ders nert know wert a celery stick his.'

An overweight man in his fifties at the next table looked at Zoe with loathing. 'Could you toast me some cheese on a baguette then?' she said, raising her voice. Let him listen!

'Zoe!'

'Certainly, madame, hif you are sure that's wert you wernt.'

'Quite sure, thanks,' said Zoe, refusing to meet the Frog's eyes.

The patron stomped back to the kitchen, devastated. He had never known anyone to refuse pigs' trotters in his life. 'I ave to hask im sermsing,' the Frog said and rushed off after him. Zoe, ignoring the other diners, opened her bag and took out a copy of *The Loves of Faustyna*, by the Irish writer Nina Fitzpatrick. She thought that Fitzpatrick might help her with the opening of her own novel—which, by now, had been either deleted again, or was in complete disarray. Zoe couldn't remember which.

'In the autumn of 1967 a cloud in the shape of human buttocks appeared over Krakow. Towards evening the cloud reddened and the angry rump drew more and more spectators into Mariacki Square.'

'Why didn't I think of that as an opening?' Zoe sighed.

A waiter arrived with her baguette, averting his eyes from the Anglo-Saxon heretic in their midst. 'Bon appetit, madame,' he said to one of the lampshades.

The Frog appeared just behind him, his face flushed with excitement—and it was at that point that Zoe saw the old scuffed pair of carpet slippers he was wearing on his feet.

'*What* are those?' she said. 'Did you wear those things all the way here?'

The Frog glanced at his feet. 'Oui,' he answered. 'Why? Wert's the preblerm?'

'You can't wear *slippers* out to *dinner*!'

'These are my father's slippers,' the Frog explained, gazing at them with pleasure. 'E bert them befur the war. E liked them so merch, e nevaire terk them erff, heven when e wers hinvited hout to dinner. E cerd nert bear changing hinto shoes. "Wert fur?" he used to say. "I ham cermfertaberl as I ham." My ferther wers a true Frenchman! Noberdy cerd horder im haround! I ham wearing is slippers hin onour erf is memory.'

There was a great scraping of chairs as the other diners rose to their feet and gave the Frog a standing ovation. 'My ferther wers hunique!' shouted the Frog, egged on by his compatriots. 'I can still see im hin his beret, driving ern the wreng side erf the road!'

He sat down misty-eyed, and a waiter rushed over with a bottle of superb red wine. 'Ern the house, monsieur!' he cried, removing the cork with aplomb.

'You have the nerve to turn your father's slippers into a symbol of la France profonde!' Zoe hissed in outrage.

'Bert herf curse! My father's slippers, pigs' trertters, leek soup, flageolet beans...erl these sings are wert makes France great!' snuffled the Frog.

'Don't weep, monsieur!' cried the owner, rushing over with an enormous plate of pigs' trotters. 'You are a great Frenchman! I, Pierre, salute you!'

The two men formally embraced.

From that moment, the Frog's emotions spiralled out

of control—and, for the first time since he and Zoe had met, he talked non-stop throughout the meal, in a mixture of French and English. Oblivious to her icy expression, he tried to express to her the beauty of what was in his mouth. But words kept failing him, and he was forced to use his tea towel to wipe the tears splashing from his eyes. The other customers wore tea towels around their necks as well, Zoe noticed. Her lips tightened and she wondered whether she had brought enough money with her to stay in a hotel.

The evening finally came to an end, and once more Pierre embraced the Frog as he and Zoe left the restaurant—waiting until Zoe had passed him before saying in a low voice, 'Au revoir, monsieur. Bon courage.'

'I understood that,' said Zoe, without turning her head.

It had begun to pour with rain and a taxi had been summoned. The Frog, still wrapped in nostalgia, shrieked snatches of old songs and intermittently wept, while the driver kept up a stream of filthy curses about the weather and the day he was born.

'You're not related by any chance?' Zoe asked the Frog.

'Erl Frenchmen are related wern way and anerther! We merst protect hourselves frem the fureign hinfidel!' he shouted in reply.

Back at the apartment, Zoe dismissed the Frog's offer

of a nightcap. 'I have never spent such an appalling evening in my life,' she told him. 'Tomorrow I'm going somewhere decent to lunch. And then I'm going to the Louvre.' She walked out of the living room without a backward glance.

'Bert Zoe! I sert we might lerk fur a new vegetaberl peeler together!' he wailed as she closed her door.

Zoe was dragged back to consciousness from the deep sleep that jet lag brings, by the sound of combat.

In between muffled French obscenities, the Frog was howling for help. With her eyes half-closed, she felt her way across the dim entrance to the living room, wrapped in a series of sarongs and the quilt from the bed. 'Waz wrong?' she croaked. 'I was fast asleep.'

'Hit's nert my ferlt! Hit hattacked me! Why can I nert ave han hernhimpeded life?'

Zoe raised her head and was confronted by an extraordinary scene. The Frog, who was stark naked, had somehow managed to entangle himself in the mosquito net and was wildly flailing his arms.

'Elp me, Zoe, befur I serffercate!'

It was the first time Zoe had seen him naked, and it was not a sight to be taken lightly. She let the quilt slip to the floor, and sat down on the edge of a chair, wondering if this was all part of a dream. Then she heard the Paris traffic with its cacophony of car horns outside.

She had never seen a photograph of Bulgakov in the nude, or Vargas Llosa, so she had no way of comparing the physiques of the men. However the Frog, not to mince matters—although this was an unfortunate verb, thought Zoe, with a flash of anguish for all those pigs dying in abattoirs for their trotters—was a size that would have made Michelangelo nod with approval.

'Oui, I ham well hindued!' shrieked the Frog, seeing the direction of her eyes. 'Pas mal, eh? Bert I wern't be merch lernger, hif you dern't get me hout erf ere!'

Belly, not too bad. A lifetime of cassoulets hadn't yet ruined the basic framework. Nice thighs. Good legs. Feet—whoops. There was a great tearing sound and the Frog fell back onto the bed dragging the mosquito net with him.

'I ate this mosquito net!' he roared, thrashing around like a giant fish in a net.

Zoe threw him a pair of scissors, conveniently lying on the table. 'Here! Cut your way out!'

'Cerdn't you cert me out, Zoe?'

'I'd rather not,' she replied, influenced in this decision by a sudden vision of the Frog's genitals springing loose as they were freed from the netting that bound them. 'I'm sure you'll manage on your own. I'm going to take a bath.'

When she returned to the living room, the Frog was sitting at the table, wrapped in Zoe's discarded quilt, and holding the remains of the mosquito net in his hands. 'I'm going out for breakfast to the cafe across the square,' she informed him.

The Frog instantly cheered up and announced that he would come too. 'I ham sterving!' he shouted. 'Hit's erlmost noon. And hexercise erlways makes me angry!'

'You will shower and shave first,' Zoe ordered. Somehow, seeing him naked, seemed to have given her the edge in their relationship.

The cafe across the square had old marble tables and tiny black-and-white photographs of men in caps fishing along the Seine. Zoe and the Frog sat over steaming bowls of coffee, after ordering pain au chocolat. It had started raining again and the chestnut trees outside began to glisten in the wet.

'This cafe lerks like the wern hin Lerndern where I hused to meet Elias Canetti,' the Frog remarked.

Zoe choked on her pastry. 'What did you say?'

'You sherdn't heat so ferst. You'll get hindigestion.'

'What did you say about Elias Canetti?'

'I said I hused to meet him hin a cafe jerst like this wern,' the Frog repeated. 'What's wreng? Are you going to be hill? Your face as terned a ferny celeur.'

'You met Elias Canetti?'

'Oui. I jerst said. When I wers living hin Amstead hin the late sixties. I wers around twenty, hin my sermmer olidays.'

Zoe felt her heart constrict. 'So you can't be forty-seven,' she stammered, trying to hide the turmoil she felt. 'More like forty-nine.'

'Bouf! I lerk years yernger!'

'Why didn't you mention Elias Canetti before?'

'Why? His hit himpertent?'

'Oh no. Of course not. You've just tossed into the conversation the fact that you used to meet one of the major literary figures of the twentieth century for casual conversation, when I had to queue at the Sydney Writers' Festival just to get a glimpse of the back of Salman Rushdie's head!' She broke off and took a series of deep breaths, trying to calm herself. The last thing she needed right now was another panic attack. This revelation of the Frog's, though, was far, far worse than taking her to eat pigs' trotters. 'What was he like?' she finally managed to ask.

'E wers very nice. E wers smerll and plermp, with a merstache, and e erlways wore a grey suit and carried a leetle leather satcherl ernder is herm.'

'What did you talk about?'

'I cannert remember now.'

'You *can't remember*?'

'It wers serch a lerng time ago, Zoe, and we terked habout so many sings. May I?' The Frog removed the pain au chocolat which Zoe was still clutching in her hands and began to eat it.

She stared blindly out of the window at the rain—a terrible thought having just crossed her mind. The one book of Canetti's she didn't own was *Notes from Hampstead: The Writer's Notes: 1954–1971*. It was too awful to contemplate. Could Canetti have immortalised the Frog somewhere in its pages? As casually as she could, Zoe asked, 'Do you have Canetti's *Notes from Hampstead* by any chance?'

'Non. I honly ave *Auto Da Fe*,' the Frog replied.

There was no time to lose. The moment they got back to Sydney she would track down a copy. 'What were you doing hanging out in Hampstead cafes, anyway?' she asked, trying to keep her voice normal. 'I thought you were meant to be an explorer.'

'I ham,' the Frog defended himself. 'I ave hexplored cafes erl hover the world. We had bettaire get moving hif we weren't to go to the Louvre befur lernch,' he added.

The waiter who had come to clear away their plates, overheard this. 'Monsieur,' he said. 'There wers a berm-scare at the Louvre this merning. You cannert go there today.'

'Dersn't hanywern hin Paris speak French hanymere?' shouted the Frog.

'A bomb-scare!' said Zoe. 'Who would bomb the Louvre?'

The waiter muttered something about foreigners and put a saucer on the table with the bill.

'There his honly wern sing to do,' announced the Frog. 'We will carry ern to lernch! I know han hexcellent brasserie near ere.'

'We've only just had breakfast!' Zoe exclaimed.

'We ave ardly heaten hanysing.'

'I warn you—'

'Relax, Zoe. This restaurant ders nert serve pigs' trertters.'

They had to make a run for it when they left the cafe, dashing around the corner and under the awnings of some shops to get out of the rain. As they did so, Zoe felt her mind go blank. A new idea for the novel which she had been turning over in her mind had been washed away by the Paris downpour.

They reached the brasserie wet and windblown. 'This is prerberbly mere your sert erf sing than mine,' he commented, as they walked inside.

Zoe looked around. Emmanuelle Beart lookalikes adorned every table and brooding Daniel Auteils stared moodily into their wineglasses, or at the breasts of the women opposite them. The main attraction, though, was a spectacular-looking woman with bright yellow hair and thigh-high red leather boots who kept exclaiming at the top of her voice, 'C'est pas vrai! C'est vrai? Oh, lalalalalalalala,' pausing over her artichoke slivers to glance from slanted eyes at every newcomer.

Her companion, whose coat was draped over his shoulders, kept leaning forward as he tantalised her with lord knows what kind of inside-Paris scandal. This was *not* a pigs' trotters kind of place.

'At last,' Zoe breathed. 'The *real* Paris.'

She was reminded of Francoise Sagan's novel *The Unmade Bed*, which followed the fortunes of bright young playwright Edouard Maligrasse, the toast of literary Paris, and the beautiful actress Béatrice Valmont, who becomes his mistress.

'"You don't eat enough, Edouard," Béatrice was saying. "Do you love me?" And he, listlessly helping himself to potatoes he had no desire for: "I love you, I've never loved anyone but you. On the other hand, I don't think I give a damn about this herring."'

Zoe looked across the table at the Frog. They had been seated against the wall, beneath clusters of tiny golden lamps, from where they had an excellent view of the other diners. Basking in the warmth and in the sidelong glances of another Frenchman just across the room, she wondered—was she beginning to be attracted, just a little, to her travelling companion? He wasn't the toast of literary Paris, nor Sydney, for that matter, and his desire for pigs' trotters was inexcusable, but he *had* spent a period of his life with Elias Canetti, and his hair had looked so good against the art nouveau architecture last night. Perhaps, the thought struck her, if his name was Edouard, it would help matters. 'Have you ever thought about changing your name?' she asked him.

The Frog, who had his nose stuck in a menu, looked up. 'Non. Why wert I?' Zoe tried to put it as delicately as she could. 'Oh, you know, "the Frog" is a bit, well, coarse.'

He preened himself. 'I like being cerlled the Frog,' he said. 'Heverywern cerlls me that. Hit means they hidentify France with me.' He returned to the entrees.

No, Zoe concluded, he wouldn't suit being called Edouard. No one who ate as much as the Frog could ever be called Edouard.

The menus arrived just as an elegant elderly couple — she wearing a wonderful hat with fur around the brim, he smoking a cigar—were seated at the next table.

'I can't imagine those two pigging out,' said Zoe sotto voce, frowning slightly as the cigar smoke drifted her way. 'I'd like to look that good when I'm their age,' she added.

'They're French, that's erl,' replied the Frog. 'Hit's genetic.'

He bent his head over his menu again. 'Ow ham I meant to decide between canard aux petis pois and hare stewed hin red wine? And there's pheasant avec braised celery as well. Wert are you aving, Zoe?'

'The onion tart.'

'Why dern't you ave the hare?'

'Because I'm having the onion tart.'

'Bert Zoe, I wernt to ave the canard aux petit pois.'

'Then have it,' Zoe told him.

'Bert I wernt to ave the hare as well—and the pheasant.'

'Well, I'm not ordering the hare or the pheasant, just because you want two main courses,' Zoe retorted. Her earlier warm feelings for the Frog were fast dissolving.

The waiter, a man in his fifties with crinkly black hair and a knowing expression, who had been hovering discreetly—or indiscreetly, in the way of Parisian waiters—during this exchange, came forward. 'We cerd, per'aps, harrange a leetle tasting plate erf heverysing ern the menu fur monsieur,' he said helpfully.

The Frog, while pleased with this suggestion, looked cross that yet another French waiter was speaking to him in English. He told the waiter this and the two men began what turned into a longer and detailed conversation. Every now and then they glanced at Zoe. She found her book, buried her head in it, and thus failed to notice the Frog slip a tiny white envelope into the waiter's hand. Soon after this their meals were served, and the Frog became his usual, effusive self.

'Per'aps there's serm ope hin life hafter erl!' he cried. He waved his glass of wine at the elderly couple, who had begun working their way respectively through two huge meals. 'Bon appetit!' he cried.

'God,' said Zoe in awe, as she watched them gobbling the beef (him) and the pheasant with braised celery (her). 'They eat as much as you do, and as fast.'

'Herf curse!' cried the Frog. 'We are French!'

The four of them finished eating their meals at the same time and, within seconds, the elderly couple summoned the waiter and ordered tarte au citron for dessert.

'Wert han hexcellent idea,' said the Frog. 'I'll horder the same fur ers.'

'I don't think I can eat another thing,' Zoe replied, trying to stifle a yawn. 'Why don't you give your stomach a rest?'

'You are terking like an Hanglo-Saxon hagain! My stermach his nert han hinvalid!'

Another yawn prevented Zoe from answering. 'I think I must still be suffering from jet lag,' she said a minute later. 'I'm feeling very sleepy.'

This remark pleased the Frog immensely. He exchanged looks with the waiter, who had come to clear away the plates. Again they had a conversation in rapid French. 'Do you mind?' said Zoe sleepily. 'Some people speak English here, you know.'

'I wers jerst telling him the recipe fur derk liver, perk and veal terrine,' the Frog said smoothly. 'Mince heverysing together and mix it theroughly with bacern, parsley, serm garlic, serm green peppercerns, two heggs, serm serlt, a grated nertmeg, black pepper and a glass erf brandy hor cognac. Preferably cognac. Then you pert it hin the fridge fur two hor three ours. Then you cerk it hin the hervern fur an hour and forty-five minutes hin a bain-marie. Let it cool dern hovernight. Next day, pert it berk hin the fridge, and leave it there fur hanerther forty-eight hours.'

'What about the measurements?' yawned Zoe.

'Bouf! You use has merch has you need!' he replied. 'I hordered the tarte au citron,' he added. 'Are you sure you dern't wernt hany?'

Zoe yawned again. 'No thanks. I feel like going back to the apartment for a siesta.'

'I sink that's a very good idea,' approved the Frog.

She missed the cunning look that crossed his face, the way he slapped the waiter on the back as they left the brasserie and the generous tip that changed hands. She was having trouble keeping her eyes open.

Outside, the rain had become a steady drizzle and the temperature had dropped. A church bell, like the one she had heard the first morning at Neutral Bay, chimed somewhere in a street nearby, a melancholy sound. Her strange fatigue deepened.

She watched the couple who had been sitting next to them at lunch totter past under an umbrella, arguing over what to have for dinner. 'We must never, ever, turn into that couple,' she remarked without thinking, gazing after them. A sudden gust of wind blew the rain into their faces.

'We erlready are that cerperl,' the Frog replied.

When she regained consciousness, she was being lifted out of a wheelchair and helped into a seat in the first-class section of a jumbo jet.

The Frog sat down next to her. He was wearing his aviator's scarf over a coat with the collar turned up to his ears, and looked very pleased with himself.

'Where are we?' said Zoe crossly. Her head was splitting. 'Why do I keep losing consciousness with you? Why do you look like a character from a John le Carre novel? And what's that smell that's clinging to your coat?'

'You sherdn't drink so merch, Zoe. I dern't know wert I ham going to do with you,' he replied, ignoring all her questions.

'WHY AM I ON A PLANE?'

'Sssh, dern't shout, you're hembarrassing me.'

Realisation dawned as a fawning male French flight attendant, young, wan, obviously impressionable, came to wipe her brow with a damp cloth. 'I don't believe it! You drugged my food!' she said. 'And to think that Madeleine once scoffed when I thought you might drug the quails the first night you cooked me dinner!'

'I wish I ad thought erf that,' remarked the Frog.

'WHY DID YOU DRUG MY FOOD?'

'It wers fur your hown good,' the Frog replied soothingly. 'We had to return to Haustralia himmediately, and I did nert wernt hany harguments.'

'We're going back to Australia?' Zoe repeated in disbelief. 'But we've only just arrived in Paris!'

'That his nert the point! We ave to go ome so that I can practise cerking my pigs' trertters hin time fur the dinner perty.'

'But you don't know how to cook pigs' trotters!'

'Oui, I do!' crowed the Frog. 'The howner erf Le Pied de Cochon showed me ow. Bert e made me premise nevaire, hever, to reveal the recipe.'

'We're going back to Sydney so that you can cook some revolting little pigs' feet?'

'Oui! I am so hexcited! Fur the ferst time hin my life, I ave had my lerky break!'

His joy was interrupted by the captain, a man with

greying hair who came and shook the Frog's hand with vigour. 'Bravo!' he exclaimed, with a quick look at Zoe. 'You do France proud, monsieur!'

'Merci,' the Frog responded. 'And erl without white chocolate mousse!'

'Incroyable!' said the captain, shaking his head.

'It's himperternt we know ow to be'ave like real Frenchmen, with erl this fureign hinvasion going ern,' the Frog continued, as the captain listened to him respectfully.

Zoe ignored this exchange. She had no idea what they were talking about, and didn't care. She was, however, getting fed up with sidelong glances from Frenchmen who otherwise didn't seem to have a civilised word to say to her. 'How did you get me through immigration when I was out cold?' she snapped when the captain had returned to the cockpit.

'I terld them you passed hout when we were making lerve. The French hundersternd these sings. That's why we were herpgraded to First Class.' He beamed at her and picked up the menu. 'Ah bon!' he said with satisfaction. 'This is merch bettaire than befur. They ave truffled pate erf derk ern the menu. Werd you like serm, Zoe?'

No answer.

'Zoe?'

'You told them I passed out while making love with

you?' repeated Zoe, when she managed to find her voice.

'Bert herf curse! Why do you sink the pilert came dern to congratulate me?'

The plane soared into the pale blue European sky and turned south-east. Zoe reached for her dark glasses. She could never invent a plot as diabolical as her life with the Frog. 'Don't speak to me for the rest of the flight.' Her voice was shaking with anger.

'That's wert you said to me ern the way hover,' the Frog reminded her amiably.

He glanced at the passenger across the aisle, who was staring their way. 'She's aving an horser's merde,' he explained, as Zoe pushed the button at the side of her seat until she was in a reclining position. 'I sink she needs a martini.'

'I wasn't wondering about that,' the passenger replied. 'I was wondering what the strange smell was.'

'I sink it's er,' the Frog replied. 'Writers sermtimes furget to wersh.'

'What does she write about?' the passenger asked, craning his neck to have a look at Zoe.

'That, monsieur,' sighed the Frog, with a genuinely worried look, turning to look at the comatose figure by his side, 'is an even bigger mystery.'

'Wake erp, Zoe! We ave to go to the supermerket right away.'

Zoe gasped and sat up. Hadn't she been pulled rudely from her sleep like this only recently? The Frog was standing in the doorway of her room, looking cross. 'What time is it?' she said groggily.

'It's erlmost two ho'clerk ern Friday hafternern.'

They had flown back into Sydney early that morning, and Zoe had gone straight to bed the moment they walked into the apartment.

'I ham sterving!' she heard the familiar refrain. 'I wers going to heat the Jesus de Lyon, bert I hate it ern the plane.'

Zoe regarded him warily, blinking in the bright Australian light. 'You ate *what* on the plane?'

'The Jesus de Lyon. Hit's a special salami we simply hadore hin France. I had two erf them strapped to my sherlders.'

'So that was the smell,' said Zoe, remembering. She had another flashback from the flight. 'That conversation you had with the captain about white chocolate mousse—what was that all about?'

'When nussing his werking—when you cannert get a worman hinto bed—feeding er white chocolate mousse husually ders the trick,' the Frog explained. 'The Hayatollah his very pleased that we are berk,' he continued, switching subjects. 'E elped me write the first draft erf the menu fur the dinner perty hern Mernday night. I rang heverywern while you were still asleep. Heverywern is cerming. Heven the Pisswomples! I sink they secretly like me very merch.'

'Why have the dinner party on Monday night? Why not tomorrow night? Or Sunday night?' Zoe asked crossly.

'Nert henerf time to prepare. There is a great deal I merst do. Hincidentally,' the Frog added, 'Howard wernts you to ring him.'

'Did you tell him why we returned so suddenly?' Zoe inquired.

'Oui.'

'And?'

'E said hernder the circumsternces, e completely hundersterd,' beamed the Frog.

There and then, Zoe decided Howard could kiss her report goodbye. She was through with being kidnapped and drugged as a result of acting as his unpaid research assistant. Fuming over the psychiatrist's treachery, she snapped, 'Why this sudden urge to shop at a supermarket? I thought you were meant to be such a gourmand.'

'I like to hinspect wert Hanglo-Saxons are erp to,' the Frog replied. 'Hand supermerkets are sermtimes very hinteresting. I buy my flageolet beans there,' he pointed out.

'Stay clerse to me,' the Frog ordered her. 'Dern't disappear.' A cold blast of air hit them as they walked inside.

Zoe ignored him.

'Leeks!' cried the Frog, throwing them into a trolley. 'We can ave soup tonight! And serm goat's cheese hin a salad with roast perk!'

'How many times do I have to tell you that I don't eat pork?' snapped Zoe. 'You know how I feel about pigs! Anyway, I feel like fish.'

'Hokay, we'll buy serm feesh jerst fur you,' the Frog replied, in a good mood because he had just spotted his favourite white Italian beans nearby. 'I lerve these leetle beans!' he cried, sweeping two dozen cans into the trolley.

Zoe trailed behind the Frog, trying to look invisible—a *writer* in a supermarket, if you please—and became increasingly irritated at the way he kept stopping to read, with an entranced expression, the labels on the food, making bizarre 'caw-caw' noises, like a crow. 'Honestly,' she said, 'anyone would think you'd never been in a supermarket before. You're behaving like a refugee from the old communist bloc.'

'Hevery time I cerm ere, it's like being bern again,' the Frog replied with fervour. He found some gherkins in a new, giant-sized jar, and almost swooned.

'I'll go and get the toilet paper,' said Zoe impatiently, leaving the Frog gazing at the gherkins with rapture.

She returned to find his mood had darkened. 'Where were you?' he shouted. 'I wers lerking fur you heverywhere!'

'You can't have been! You're standing exactly where I left you.' Zoe snorted.

'That his nert the point!' roared the Frog. 'I cannert ave you disappearing erl hover the place!'

Zoe tossed the toilet paper in the trolley. 'I ate that toilet paper,' the Frog said, retrieving it and pointing in an aggrieved fashion at its environmentally-friendly label. 'It urts my berm.'

A girl in her twenties with jagged green hair and a boy of about the same age—both clad in green leggings and 'Save the Tree' T-shirts—passed by and looked at him with utter contempt.

Zoe snatched the toilet paper from the Frog and shoved it on a shelf next to the gherkins.

'You cern't do that!' cried the Frog, outraged. 'This is a supermerket. You ave to ave serm horder!' He took the toilet paper and stalked off to put it back where it belonged.

Zoe commandeered the trolley and headed towards the health food section. She was tossing tofu on top of corn chips, when an anguished howl started in the distance. 'Where ave you disappeared to? Why do you keep *habanderning* me?'

The Frog found Zoe and grabbed the trolley off her. He began forcing a passage through the other shoppers. 'Hout erf my way!' he bellowed. 'I dern't wernt to be ere the hentire day!'

'May I ask where we are going now?' Zoe asked him, as she dodged around angry customers.

'To the feesh-counter, to hinspect the poissons.'

'Why don't you buy the fish from the fish shop? I thought you said you never bought fish from the supermarket.'

'I merst do my duty as a Frenchman!' declared the Frog. 'This his himperative!' He reached the fish counter then staggered back with a look of horror. 'This his a dersgrace!' he shouted. 'I cannert terlerate serch a situation! You know your feesh his dead?' he ranted at the assistant, pointing to some formerly blue-eyed cod, now with cataracts. 'I cannert heven buy these leetle werns ere,' he added, indicating some hopeless sardines, 'ertherwise I will be very hill. And regard that tuna! And the trout! They lerk like they ave cholera! Wert do you sink appened to erl these leetle feesh?'

'I dunno,' the fish-counter assistant said. 'I don't catch them.'

The Frog turned to Zoe. 'Wert kind erf world his hit, when yerng people don't know ow to recergnise an ealthy feesh?'

The fish-counter assistant, who had a nose-ring, and acne, looked bored.

'I ave to ask you sermsing,' the Frog went on in a more gentle tone. 'Ave you hever heaten feesh hor vegetaberl soup hin your life?'

'Nuh,' the assistant replied. 'Oi never eat vegetables. Like, they're for old people. Oi like hamburgers, meself.' He looked put out at the length of this speech.

The Frog seemed to be on the point of fainting. 'I wernt to see the manager,' he choked.

'I'm already here, sir,' said a voice behind him. 'I was alerted by security.' The Frog turned and saw a young man in his late twenties, brimming with confidence. The manager had recently completed a course in supermarket management, as well as a parallel course in behavioural psychology, specially designed to calm customers with emotional problems, and he was keen to try it out. He smiled at the Frog. 'Isn't it a lovely day?'

'I ave no idea. Wert a ridiculers remark. Wern day is merch the same has anerther. Did you know you hemploy sermwern who as nevaire heaten soup?'

'It's not essential for the job, sir,' the manager replied, with another beatific smile.

'Why do you keep smiling like that?' the Frog demanded. 'Are you trying to make a mernkey hout erf me? Your feesh counter represents the hend erf civilisation!'

The manager's smile faltered. He hadn't done civilisation in his supermarket studies. He wondered if the Frog was armed.

'Erl your feesh is putrid,' the Frog went on. 'Aven't you eard erf cholera?'

The manager turned white. So that was it. 'Are you the new health inspector, sir?'

'You cerd say that,' the Frog replied. 'I serggest you throw erl your feesh haway himmediately.'

The manager bowed. 'Right away, sir.' He signalled frantically to the assistant to get rid of the lot. 'Is there anything else we can do for you?'

'Oui. Sterp erl those orriberl hannouncements habout

price certs hover the lerdspeaker. I cannert hear myself sink!'

'Yes, sir.'

'And sterp moving sings around erl the time! I can nevaire find wert I am lerking fur!'

The Frog took the shopping straight into the kitchen. 'I am serry,' he said to Zoe, 'bert I dern't feel like cerking hanymere. I ham too herpset habout the feesh. Ow habout serm poached heggs tonight hinstead?'

'Fine,' said Zoe. 'I didn't really want to eat much, anyway.'

'I ham revising the menu fur the dinner party and wernt to be erlone.' He locked the door behind him.

Zoe went back to bed and slept for the rest of the afternoon. It was dusk when she woke. The phone was ringing in the living room. She went through and picked it up. It was Max, ringing to speak to the Frog. 'He's locked in the kitchen,' Zoe replied.

'Do you mind telling him I'm on the phone? Madeleine's out, and I'm trying to make leek soup.'

Zoe banged on the kitchen door. 'Phone call for Pol Pot!' she cried.

The door swung open and the Frog burst into the living room, brandishing some sheets of paper. 'I sink I know wert I ham going to cerk!' he announced. 'Leek soup to stert, ferllowed by a rabbit hin red wine, serm quails, a leetle beef bourguignon—you'll ave a leetle, Zoe—lamb with flageolet beans, strawberry romanov, hatlantic salmon, poussins hin terragern serce, a cheese souffle, a trout, coq au vin, creme caramel, my famous potatoes hin goose fat, and then,' cried the Frog, sweeping Zoe into his arms, 'I will bring hout the pigs' trertters ern my grandmerther's big, white serving plate!'

'Max is on the phone for you,' said Zoe, extracting herself from the Frog's embrace. 'You can tell him about your utterly ridiculous menu. On Monday night I'm going to warn everyone that you drug people's food.'

She handed him the phone and went back to her room, just in time to take a call on her mobile. She had left it on, hoping Ian would phone. She was always galvanised into action after a conversation with her publisher. A phone call from him was just what she needed to unblock her literary arteries. Only amateurs got writer's block.

It *was* Ian! Fantastic! She could feel a new opening for her novel coming on already.

'Zoe, you *are* there. I knew your message about going to Paris was just a joke.'

'It wasn't a joke. We did go there.'

'No writer goes to Paris for forty-eight hours. Are you sure you're not confusing fact with fiction? So how is the novel going?'

'Brilliant!'

'Good. Let's have lunch on Sunday. I've booked at that new place at Circular Quay. Bring everything you've written. I'll have a look at it between courses.'

'The thing is, Ian—'

'See you at 1 p.m. Sharp,' he said, and hung up.

The new idea that had blossomed when Ian rang had now vanished. Zoe sped into the living room and made herself a martini. The Frog was nowhere to be seen. 'Help me, Proust!' she begged. But there was not even the faintest glimmer of an idea from the master. 'Fine!' said Zoe, fed up with their one-sided relationship. 'In that case, I'm going to make myself so drunk I'll be able to call myself a recovering novelist for the rest of the year!' She made another martini and tossed it back. And another. Nothing. Her mind was as clear as crystal. It dawned on her that—yes, this was the sign she had been waiting for. Proust had made it possible for her to drink martinis without losing her ability to write! As she stood there in the living room in awe, she felt a new idea forming. It was fuzzy, but it was there.

Zoe rushed back to her room. She shut the door, took her laptop from her bag, and began writing for her life.

The following morning the door opened and the Frog walked in with a cup of coffee and a bowl of leek soup. 'Breakferst!' he announced. 'You didn't heat your poached heggs lerst night. I left them ern a plate houtside the door. You were snoring so loudly, I didn't dare come hin. Ave you ridden your hexercise bike this merning?'

Zoe glared at him from out of red-rimmed eyes. 'It's none of your business whether I have or haven't,' she slurred. She had got a quarter of the new novel written before passing out. It was now a rich pulsating tale, full of magic realism, about a woman writer drinking herself to death in a cafe in Paris whose patron, a distant cousin of Proust's, turns into a trout and swims away through the city's gutters.

'My room is off-limits to you when I'm writing, just like your kitchen is off-limits to me when you're cooking. The solitude of a writer is not something to be taken lightly. And I don't snore.'

'Really, Zoe, why are you be'aving so hatrociously these days? Ave you ad a chat to your doctor habout your ermones?'

'My hormones, like my writing, my exercise routine and everything else about me, are none of your business!' Zoe shouted. 'And another thing. As I keep trying to tell you, hunger is *essential* for the writer's creative tension!'

'Cerdswellerp!' the Frog shouted back. 'You're herbviously aving hanerther horser's merde! I'll leave you to it. Heat your soup. I'm going to go sherpping fur your dinner!'

'For God's sake, we shopped yesterday afternoon! Why are you going shopping again?'

'There is nevaire hanysing to heat hin this ouse, that's why!'

Zoe ate the soup and then wrote twenty sentences in quick succession. A personal best for her. The problem was, in the clear light of day, she wasn't sure her new plot worked any more. But she had to show Ian something or else he'd stop the dribble of money from her advance. She ploughed on and was deep in her work when her mobile rang.

'So,' said a voice at the other end of the line, 'tonight we are aving poussins with terragern serce and potatoes hin goose fat, hokay?'

'Okay,' said Zoe, and the phone went dead.

Half an hour later, the phone rang again.

'Merde! Serm kind erf *cretin* as taken erl the poussins! So ternight we're aving a poached salmern and potatoes hin goose fat, hif I can find hany decent salmern!'

Zoe returned to her novel. Perhaps the woman writer should be a transsexual. A religious transsexual. Yes, that was more promising. The mobile rang for a third time. 'I sought you premised to take me hout fur dinner,' said a doleful voice.

'Oh, why not!' she cried, giving up. 'At least it means you'll stop ringing me!'

'Can I cherse where to go?'

'Of course. But don't try anything funny.'

'I wernt to heat Harmenian fishcakes. There's a very good Harmenian restaurant hin Kings Cross. When shall we go? I ham very angry!'

'It's only eleven o'clock in the morning,' Zoe pointed out.

'Is that erl? It cannert be! Bouf! Per'aps I sherd go and ave lernch with Max.'

'Good idea. I'll see you later,' said Zoe, and hung up.

She wrote all afternoon, stopping only to nick some lines from Jorge Luis Borges. The plot was finally working. At 7 p.m. her mobile started ringing. 'I cannert wait any lernger! I'm growing weaker by the minute!'

Zoe checked her word count. Two thousand, one hundred and fifty-six words. That should keep Ian happy. He was a slow reader.

'Okay,' she said, 'let's go.'

The Frog insisted on driving and she let him, too tired to argue. 'I wernt to heat Harmenian fishcakes,' he explained, as they drove the back way through Woolloomooloo and up the hill to the Cross, 'becurse I ham sinking erf perting them ern the menu ern Mernday night. I wernt to find hout ow they're cerked.'

'Don't you think you've got enough courses?'

'You can nevaire ave enerf curses!' shouted the Frog. 'People ave to go ome sterffed to the gulls!'

'Gills. I hope you booked. It's Saturday night.'

'Bouf! I nevaire berk! I referse to berk! Hif they dern't ave a taberl, hit's their preblerm!'

He suddenly slammed on the brakes, and the Peugeot skidded towards a pedestrian crossing. 'Lerk!' the Frog said hoarsely. 'A miracerl of creation!'

Zoe looked. A gorgeous young woman, wearing a sequined bra and a skirt designed for a four-year-old, had just stepped off the pavement on their right. As she began to saunter across the road, eating an ice-cream and dragging an out-sized bag behind her, the Frog clutched the steering wheel tighter. 'Lerk at zose legs!' he croaked. 'I ave nevaire seen serch a magnificernt pair erf legs hin my life!'

He drooled like a pervert hiding behind the bushes on a nude beach. 'Why dern't you dress like that, Zoe?'

'Because I'm not a bimbo.'

The Frog banged the steering wheel in despair. 'Why do wormen herlways get heverysing so wreng?' he complained. 'Wert his *wrerng* with bimbos! I lerve the way they dress! Hat least they dern't dress hin blerk erl the time. They wear ferny leetle clothes that make me smile. Erther wormen,' he added pointedly, 'are jerst jealous.'

'Other women,' answered Zoe, 'don't show their pantyline.'

A long line of motorists, forced to a standstill behind them, began to thump their horns. 'Cretins! Barbarians!' shrieked the Frog. 'Wert are they doing ern the road?' He twisted his head around, trying to catch one more glimpse of the vision as she threaded her way through the other pedestrians. Soon she was reduced to a bobbing head in a crowd.

'There's nevaire hany perking!' he continued to bawl, as they drove in vain up and down the side-streets.

'Try the alley over there,' suggested Zoe, pointing towards a narrow lane with rubbish. 'It has a certain Bret Easton Ellis appeal about it.'

'We'll prerberly get mergged!' raged the Frog. 'Jerst my lerk, when we go hout fur my berthday!'

They found a parking spot in the alley, outside a run-down hotel with barred windows and a brawny bouncer slouching out the front. He flashed his knuckle-dusters at them as they passed, then turned to talk to some unseen figure in the doorway.

'I'm herlways ferced to werk fer miles!' whined the Frog. 'We sherd ave stayed at ome.'

'You know perfectly well that the restaurant is just around the corner. We saw it when we drove past before,' said Zoe. 'Besides, the exercise will do you good.'

'Did *you* ride your hexercise bike terday?' the Frog countered, as they stepped over a loudly snoring man in a dirty tracksuit.

'You asked me that before, and I told you,' said Zoe. 'I ride it when you're not around, that's all.'

They had walked into the main part of the Cross with its extraordinary floating pavement population of buskers, backpackers, tourists, street artists, drunks, hustlers, hoods, rent-boys, junkies, drug dealers, prostitutes, beggars, eccentrics and perfectly ordinary locals.

'Shall we ave a drink?' the Frog suggested, waving

his arm at one of the sleaziest bars on the strip, which was open to the street.

'You must be joking!' said Zoe. 'Someone got shot in there the other week!'

'Bouf! I ave herlways met very hinteresting people hin that leetle bar,' scoffed the Frog. Sure enough, as he spoke, a couple of swarthy men doing business on their mobile phones, hailed him from their table. 'Bonjour, Monsieur Frog!' they shouted, gold rings flashing on their fingers.

The Frog raised a hand in salute. 'They gave me the name erf the best restaurant hin Bogota,' he said fondly, once he and Zoe had walked past.

'I can't believe the calibre of the people you know,' Zoe commented coldly, as the Frog continued to be hailed by an assortment of scruffy characters. 'I suspect that since you arrived in Sydney, you've spent half your time hanging out in sleazy bars.'

'Herf curse. Ow else am I going to learn about people hin Haustralia?' said the Frog, surprised. 'That's wert you sherd be doing too, Zoe. You're a writer. Writers are meant to see wert real life his. You spend too merch time hin your room. You need to get hout mere.'

'I have a very rich interior life, thank you very much,' said Zoe. 'I don't need to hang out with the lowlife in order to write a novel.'

They reached the Armenian restaurant but there

wasn't a single unoccupied table. 'I cannert believe hit!' the Frog exploded, when the owner confirmed that restaurant was booked out. '*Why* are you berked hout? Where did erl these people cerm frem?'

'It's Saturday night,' the owner said shortly. 'You should have made a reservation.'

'Told you so,' said Zoe.

'Sank you, Zoe. I dern't need your hinpert right now. Hin that case,' the Frog went on haughtily, addressing the restaurant owner, 'I werd like the recipe fur the feesh cakes.'

'Impossible,' said the owner. 'It's a secret.' He turned away to take a phone call.

The Frog drooped and walked back into the street looking as if the world had ended. 'I can nevaire ave wert I wernt!'

'Well, what about the restaurant opposite?' Zoe suggested. 'It keeps getting good reviews. Why don't we try it?'

'I ave tried it!' roared the Frog. 'Max and Madeleine terk me there after I harrived hin Sydney! I had to demand mere food to fill erp my plate!'

'Well, I don't want to stand on the pavement all night being jostled by the riff-raff,' said Zoe. 'Let's go to the noodle bar on the next corner. I've been with Ian and it's very good. Lots of authors who live locally eat there.'

'Bouf! Wert werd a *perblisher* know about food,'

muttered the Frog in his most disparaging manner. 'I dern't feel like heating noddles,' he continued to complain, as they walked through the door. 'And I dern't like sitting hon sterls,' he grizzled. 'I *ate* sterls. My feets ave nowhere to go.'

He demonstrated what he meant by falling off his stool the moment he sat down. 'That's noddle bars fur you!' he bellowed from the floor. 'And why hisn't there a wine list?'

Zoe hissed at him. 'Get back on your stool now! Are you trying to embarrass me on purpose? What happens if a book reviewer comes in?'

'It's worse than being ern the plane!' retorted the Frog, holding his breath in an exaggerated manner as he squeezed back between her stool and his.

The owner of the noodle bar had been watching this performance with narrow eyes. He went over and thrust a menu in front of each of them. There was a hint of violence in his movements.

'I was here the other week. With my publisher,' Zoe told the man, desperate for him to realise that at least *she* was civilised.

'Ready to eat?' the owner snapped. His hostile expression didn't change. He took their orders and went straight into the kitchen, reappearing five minutes later with two steaming bowls. The Frog underwent a dramatic personality change. 'Isn't it nice to ave noddles?' he cried. 'Termerrow, I merst buy a wok! I wernder if you cerd stir-fry noddles hin goose fat? Ole!' he cried, twirling his chopsticks over his shoulder.

As he bent over his bowl in ecstasy, two well-groomed young men in jeans and tight white T-shirts walked into the noodle bar and sat down on the other side of the Frog. They began talking about the weekend, and Zoe, who wasn't taking much notice, became aware that the Frog was listening to their conversation with intense interest.

'Hexcuse me,' he said to them before she could stop him. 'I cerdn't elp earing wert you were saying. I ham a Frenchman, and I ham trying to learn your language, becurse I like you very merch. It werries me when I dern't hunderstand the meanings erf werds. Can you tell me wert you meant when you said you spent the hafternoon permping Irene?'

The two young men collapsed with mirth. 'Pumping iron,' one of them said finally. 'At the gym!' they spluttered. 'Say it again!' they cried with delight.

'They sink I'm ferny,' beamed the Frog, once he had turned back to Zoe. 'Why ave you pert your dark glasses ern? Ow strange you are. Nevaire mind,' he added, taking pity on her. 'Sink erf me as a piece erf theatre.'

The streets were even more packed with people when they left the noodle bar. A woman dressed in leather with a fierce expression on her face strode past them, tearing pieces from a takeaway chicken and throwing them on the ground. 'Wert a waste,' said the Frog, shaking his head. 'I think she as lerst er merble. You dern't want to ave jerst wern glass erf wine and watch the scene?' he asked Zoe wistfully, as they passed the place where his acquaintances from Bogota had been drinking.

'I've seen more than enough for one night, thanks,' said Zoe, averting her eyes from a tribe of vacant-eyed streetkids who were drifting across the road. 'I want to get back to what really matters—my novel.'

They had just reached their alley when a voluptuous young woman wearing a denim bra, something that looked like cling wrap over a G-string and stilettos— this time there was no mistaking her profession— tottered past them. Her hair was short and spiky and her cherry-coloured lipstick had been applied with reckless indifference to the shape of her mouth. One of her heels suddenly broke and she collapsed into the gutter, cursing the shoe shop.

'I know jerst ow you feel!' cried the Frog, stepping over the broken shoe and gazing with compassion at its owner. 'Nussing hever werks. You ave to struggerl and struggerl hin this life. Wert's your name?'

'Viola,' said the prostitute shortly. 'What's it to you?'

'Viola. Wert a lervely name! I like hit very merch! Viola, I ave the perfect remedy! Hit's the honly sing

I really believe hin. Elp er hout erf the gerttaire, Zoe,' ordered the Frog, hurrying off to the car.

Viola squinted after him. 'Help me out of the what?' She raised herself with difficulty on one elbow and slapped at Zoe's proffered hand.

'We're only trying to help you,' Zoe said stiffly, stepping back.

Viola muttered something rude and kicked a beer bottle lying close by. 'You work around here?' she asked. Her implication was clear.

'Certainly not. I'm writing a novel,' Zoe replied.

'So'm I,' the woman replied. She coughed violently and scratched at her leg. 'What's your novel about?' she asked.

Zoe hesitated. She didn't see why she should be forced to stand in an alley explaining her novel to a whore.

'I said, what's it about?' Viola asked her again.

'It's conceptual,' Zoe replied in a cool tone. 'It explores the possibility of plot.'

'Conceptual,' Viola repeated.

'And yours?' Zoe inquired, suspecting the prostitute's talk of writing a novel was nothing but fantasy.

'Sex and death,' Viola answered. 'But you'd probably expect that, in my trade. It's extremely plot-driven—my novel, I mean—with lots of bestseller angles. People fucking themselves silly in swimming pools, or being pushed off cliffs and stuff. You gotta tell a story. You know, like Colleen McCullough or Bryce Courtenay. Jesus—can they write.'

'I don't think you really understand what proper literature is,' Zoe said, appalled.

'But I do,' Viola told her. 'You ever read George Orwell?' Sitting up, her legs askew, she quoted, '"Anyone able to hold a pen can write a fairly good novel of the unpretentious kind, if only at some period of his life he has managed to escape from literary society. There is no lack nowadays of clever writers; the trouble is that such writers are so cut off from the life of their time as to be unable to write about ordinary people." Orwell said that. He's got a point there, don't you think?'

For one wild moment Zoe wondered if the whole scene was a set-up. Had the Frog arranged the encounter with Viola to prove that mixing with the demi-monde was what she needed as a writer? 'Where do you write?' she asked Viola, less confidently.

'They let me keep a laptop,' Viola answered, jerking her head towards the seedy hotel further down the alley. 'Sometimes I do a house call, like just now. But usually I can tap in a few thousand words between jobs. Grab every opportunity, that's what I say.'

She was about to go on, but was cut short by the Frog's return. ''Ere it is,' he said, holding a thermos out to Viola. 'It's leek soup,' he beamed. 'I erlways keep serm hin the car hin case erf hemergencies. It will elp you feel bettaire about your shoe. Lerk, hit's nice and ot.'

Viola pulled herself to her feet, waving away the thermos in alarm. 'What the fuck is that?' she demanded. 'Are you a sicko or what?'

'Mais non, I ham nert a seeko. Hit's leek soup,' the Frog replied, bewildered. 'Aven't you hever ad leek soup befur?'

The prostitute backed away from him. 'Keep that stuff away from me!' she warned. She poked around in her bag and produced a card.

'Here,' she said, thrusting it at the Frog. 'Forget about leek soup. What you need is a good massage. Call this number and ask for Viola.' She glanced at Zoe. 'Y'can come too, if y'want. Read my novel while you're waiting. Y'might pick up a plot twist or two.'

'I don't think that's even a remote possibility,' Zoe answered.

'Suit yourself,' said Viola. She turned her attentions back to the Frog. 'Better get back to work. Every day's like winning a little war, right? Civilisation has gone to hell and humanity isn't going anywhere, but I can take you to the moon.'

'I sink you are gergess,' sighed the Frog, looking deep into her eyes.

'Au revoir, mate,' said Viola with a chuckle. She limped off, holding her broken shoe.

The Frog gazed after her. 'Wert a worman! Lerk at

those legs. Wert a pity she did nert wernt my leek soup.'

He was unusually quiet during the trip back to Neutral Bay. Zoe was driving, which helped, but it was clear he had something on his mind. 'I sink I am going ter merld er,' he announced, once they were back at the apartment. 'She as the merst amazing berdy, dern't you sink?'

'What about your first love, with the ice-cream?'

'Bouf! Viola is far mere hinteresting!'

This was too much for Zoe. 'As if it wasn't bad enough standing around in alleys trying to make conversation with a tart,' she snapped, 'now you want her to come over here and take off what few clothes she had on, and parade around in our kitchen!'

'*My* kitchen, Zoe, *my* kitchen. I sink I'll ring er himmediately!' He moved towards the phone.

Zoe grabbed his arm. 'All right,' she said, steeling herself. 'I'll do it.'

'Do wert, Zoe?'

'I'll let you make a mould of me. Right now. Tonight.'

'You're sure habout this?'

'Quite sure.'

'Ow merverllous,' said the Frog. 'I knew you werd let me merld you sooner er later. Ow cerd you resist? Bert I'd wish you'd given me mere notice. Nevaire mind. I'll go and mix serm plaster. You can take your clothes erf now, hif you like.'

'I'll try to control myself until you're ready,' said Zoe.

She waited by the kitchen door as the Frog busied himself pouring measures of water and plaster into a plastic mixing bowl on the table. He beckoned her in, indicating that she should stand on the sheet he had spread out on the floor.

'Erry erp,' he instructed her. 'The plerster wern't wait. Throw your clothes hover the bain-marie.' For someone who had done nothing except try to seduce her since she had moved in, he seemed to be taking it all a bit seriously.

Zoe unbuttoned and unzipped without looking at him. The truth was, a mould of her torso showcased in the window of the city's best bookshop would be great publicity. The novelist and her navel. Eat your heart out, Isabel Allende.

'I'm ready,' she said, stepping out of her knickers.

The Frog walked around her, peering at her body this way and that. 'I wers right habout your berk. And your pubic air his nert bad fur han Hanglo-Saxon, although per'aps it cerd do with a trim.'

'Do you mind?' glared Zoe.

'Your berm is cervered hin little bermp-gooses. Hit reminds me erf the derk with horange and cherry serce that my grandmerther hused to make. Shall we hopen a bottle of champagne?'

'No thanks. Just get on with it, will you?' said Zoe.

'Hokay,' said the Frog, and he began to rub great

handfuls of plaster over her body. 'You know wert I ham sinking habout, Zoe?' he asked her as he finished her shoulders and started on her breasts.

'Rodin's *Pygmalion and Galatea*?'

'A dessert called Petites Iles Flottant. It means leetle floating islands. They're like meringues, and they float hin vanilla cersterd avec caramel ern terp. Hit merst be your nipples, Zoe, that are giving me these ideas. Are you doing hit ern perpose?'

'I'm not doing anything on purpose,' said Zoe. The feeling of the Frog's hands on her body was unexpectedly erotic.

'I serppose I will jerst ave to concentrate ern your ribcage.'

'Please do.'

'You ave a beautiferl ribcage, Zoe.'

'I'm beginning to feel giddy,' Zoe interrupted. 'I'm very claustrophobic. I didn't realise how trapped I'd feel, covered in plaster as it hardens.'

'You'll be fine,' the Frog soothed her. His fingers brushed her pubic hair. Zoe made no comment. She wasn't going to encourage him. Besides, he was probably thinking about Viola.

'You know,' said the Frog thoughtfully, gazing at her thighs, 'I sink we sherd buy serm derks and keep them ern the balcony. And serm geese. Then we cerd ave our hown pate de fois gras. Wert do you sink?'

'I think I'm going to faint,' Zoe said a little desperately, as a yellow mist appeared before her eyes.

'You cannert faint!' the Frog shouted. 'You'll break the mould! You ad bettaire ave serm whisky. I ave a bottle andy fur medicinal purposes.'

Grabbing it from the side of the bench, he poured the alcohol down her throat. 'You're giddy becurse you didn't ave a drink tonight,' he admonished her.

'That's enough,' said Zoe, pushing the whisky away. 'I feel much better, thanks.' She paused. 'There's that strange smell again. What *is* it?'

'You're herlways smelling sermsing strange. I ave no idea wert you're terking habout,' the Frog replied. He took a swig from the bottle, and then leaned back against the wall, surveying his handiwork. 'I find you mere hexciting than warm fig tart,' he pronounced.

'Thank you. I had no idea. How long do I have to stand like this?'

He gently touched the plaster enclosing her body. 'Hanerther three minutes,' he decided. It didn't seem long, but the yellow mist reappeared without warning in front of Zoe's eyes and, as hard as she tried to stand motionless, the muse in her suddenly gave up.

'Hokay,' yelled the Frog, as she began to sway. 'We take the cast erf now!'

Somehow he managed to remove it before Zoe crumpled up altogether. 'Ernestly, Zoe,' he said, cradling the mould as he examined it for cracks, 'I ad no hidea you were so fragile. You're heither weeping or fainting. Why don't you ave a shower and then go and sit hout ern the balcony and get serm fresh air?'

'Yes, I will,' said Zoe shakily.

The Frog continued to work on the mould for a while longer with a palette knife. He glanced out the window and saw Zoe with her head bent over a book, at the table beneath the bougainvillea. She was reading in the pool of light coming from the kitchen window. 'You'll ruin your eyes,' he called to her. 'Why dern't you read hinside.'

There was no answer. He walked out on the balcony. Zoe hid the book she was reading behind her back.

'Zoe? Wert's the mattaire? Are you aving han horser's merde hagain?'

Zoe looked at him. She was very pale. 'Something like that,' she replied.

When Zoe reminded the Frog next morning that she was having lunch with her publisher, he was furious. 'Bert I wers going to cerk bleu swimmer crab for lernch! Wert a waste erf time!'

'Be reasonable,' said Zoe. 'You have Tiggi, I have Ian. We all have our obligations.'

'Ziggi. Bouf! We will ave the crabs fur dinner. You'll need serm real food this hevening.'

Zoe didn't get back from lunch until almost five o'clock. She went straight into the living room where the Frog was just putting down the phone, grabbed his beloved French-English dictionary from off the bookshelves, and hurled it at his head.

'Wert wers that fur?' cried the Frog, ducking.

'Two things. Firstly, when I'm having lunch with my publisher and his mobile rings, I don't expect him to have to pass on, with a bewildered expression, the following message: "Why didn't sermwern remember to buy mere bluddy vegetaberl bouillon powder?" And secondly, how *dare* you install a secret camera in my room, and then send him the tape of me sitting on my exercise bike reading Jeffrey Archer?'

'I did it fur your hown good!' said the Frog self-righteously. 'I sert Yarn sherd know that when you're meant to be writing, you are sitting ern your bike reading. Hat this rate, you'll nevaire finish writing your noverl.'

'It's Ian, not Yarn. Can't you ever pronounce anything correctly?'

'Ave a drink,' the Frog said soothingly, pouring her a glass of wine. 'Writers are their hown worst henemies. You will sank me later ern. Did Yarn like the noverl sew far?'

Zoe's face crumpled and she sank down onto the sofa with a look of pure misery.

'Zoe! Wert's the mattaire?'

'He couldn't understand it! He said the whole thing needs rethinking. I'm so depressed,' she said in a hollow voice. 'You have no idea how awful my life has been for the past two days.' She checked herself. 'I mean, this afternoon. Ian thinks my novel should be more plot-based. I pointed out that it was, now, but he said, "Call that a plot?" I was so humiliated!'

'So ow wers lernch?' he asked.

'You already asked me that. I told you, Ian wants me to reconceptualise the narrative yet again!'

'I wers terking habout the food.'

'How stupid of me. How could I have ever imagined you meant anything else? I had pan-kissed scallops and a Caravaggio-inspired tuna carpaccio. Ian had a symphony of zucchini sausages curled around a polenta emboldened by stewed peppers.'

'Ave you lerst your merble?'

'That's what it said on the menu.'

'Himbeciles!'

'I invited Ian to the dinner party tomorrow night, by the way. He's curious to meet you,' said Zoe.

'Bon! This will be han himperternt hevening hin is life!'

'The problem is,' Zoe continued, 'I have to get straight back to work so that I'll have something new for him when he arrives.'

'Himperssiberl!' cried the Frog. 'First sing hin the merning, we merst drive deep hinto the cerntryside to buy serm special, horganically corn-fed chickens frem the best free-range ferm hin New South Wales! We merst leave hearly! Has soon has we get erp!'

'Oh God,' Zoe groaned. 'This dinner party is going to be a nightmare. Why don't we just go to the markets? I hate going too far from the city. No one has ever heard of Ryzsard Kapuscinski and people have tattoos. And there are no real cafes in the bush.'

'You nevaire go to cafes hanyway!' the Frog shouted. 'I do! That's why I met Canetti and you didn't! And hanyway, we ave to go to this ferm. The poulets I buy frem the markets are too smerll. Heven the quails were hundersized lerst time. This dinner perty is to celebrate hour relationship. Can't you sink erf me fur a change? I did erl the rest erf the sherpping while you were aving lernch fur hours and hours with Yarn. Merde! I furgert the potatoes. I merst go and buy serm straight haway!'

'But you're always buying potatoes!' Zoe exclaimed in disbelief. 'What do you do with them all? We certainly don't eat enough to justify the huge numbers you keep coming home with.'

'You can nevaire buy henerf potatoes!' he barked, picking up his car keys. 'You merst buy mere hevery day! Dern't you listen to the news? Sermwern his ording herl the potatoes hin Sydney! It's han houtrage!' With that, he left the apartment. In his haste to leave he had forgotten to secure the kitchen. Zoe realised that this was her opportunity. Finally, she could break into his secret cupboard to see what it actually contained.

She walked towards the cupboard in question—there was no mistaking it, it was padlocked and had a picture of a skull and crossbones pinned to it. The stench she kept mentioning to the Frog wafted towards her.

She had no idea where the Frog kept the key. A few good bangs with the bottom of a frying pan should be enough to demolish the cupboard door, and she could always blame the damage on the Ayatollah.

Zoe got out the Frog's heaviest pan. Three solid blows. The door erupted off its hinges and she was hit by a wall of potatoes.

Potatoes rolled in all directions across the floor. She took the torch which the Frog kept on the bench and shone it into the darkness of the cupboard. No wonder Sydney had a potato shortage. There were desirees, king edwards, sebagos, pontiacs and nicolas. Small chats and large idaho potatoes. There were small, elegant yellow spuds with unblemished skin, and wholesome pink scrubbed numbers with interesting black eyes as well as the kipfler potatoes the Frog loved to have with fish.

The thing that Zoe found so terrifying, however, was that the potatoes looked new. No, not all. She pointed the torch deeper into the cupboard and saw the old guard in the shadows. Some were so shrivelled that they looked like archaeological discoveries. A few had started to rot, causing the smell which she had been wondering about ever since she had moved in.

Holding her nose, she plucked out the smelliest spuds and threw them in the garbage. Then she rolled the remaining tubers onto the kitchen floor, cleaned out the cupboard and began to do a head count. She was still counting when she heard the Frog's key trying to open the front door. Frantically she began stuffing them back in the cupboard, cursing herself for not watching the time.

'Wert appened ere? Wert criminerl broke hinto my secret potato store? Why is my cerpberd door destroyed?' The Frog hadn't shaved that day and his escaped-criminal impression was very convincing.

'The door just exploded. It blew right off its hinges. Are you sure the cat hasn't been trying to make a bomb?' Zoe asked.

The Frog looked at her and then he saw the frying pan with its brand new dent. His *new* frying pan with the brand new dent! 'Ow cerd you!' he roared. 'You're *spying* ern my potatoes! I knew this werd appen. This is why I didn't wernt you hin the kitchen hin the first place.'

'Have you any idea how many potatoes you have in that cupboard?' Zoe demanded, going on the defensive. 'I was up to three hundred and seventy-eight, and still counting. And that doesn't include those I had to throw away.'

'So wert?' bawled the Frog. 'Wert makes you sink

potatoes sherdn't be herllowed to grow erld?' He picked up the ones that were soft in all the wrong places and placed them tenderly on the bench. 'I lerve my potatoes erlmost as merch as I lerve gherkins and goose fat. These are himpertant sings hin life. Tonight, I ham going to turn some lerky potatoes hinto frites, to heat with the bleu swimmer crabs.'

'They're just boring little root vegetables, and you're completely insane!' Zoe snapped. She went to her room—which was fast becoming her refuge—and spent the next hour or so staring at her laptop, waiting to be called on her mobile to dinner. No call came. Perhaps the Frog had taken the blue swimmer crabs and given them to Max and Madeleine, to punish her for her behaviour. Or perhaps he had released the crabs into the harbour in a rage.

When she ventured forth the Frog was on the balcony, speaking in unusually calm tones for someone mad. 'So, now you know erl habout the Napoleonic Wars,' he was saying. 'Werd you like serm mere to heat?'

Zoe swiftly crossed the living room. The Ayatollah could bloody well dine elsewhere tonight. But it wasn't the cat who was sitting on the balcony, happily sharing a plate of fritters with the Frog. It was a possum with a pink nose, pink paws and eyes like Anais Nin.

'What are you feeding that creature?' she snapped.

'This persserm happreciates food very merch, nert

like serm people I cerd mention. She knows that food ders nert grow ern plates. When she as finished er fritter, I ham going to make er han honion and cream tart.'

'Where are the blue swimmer crabs?'

'I turned them hinto the fritters the persserm and I ave jerst heaten.'

'You gave blue swimmer crab to a possum?'

'Why nert? You ad pan-pissed scerllerps avec your publisher.'

'That's got nothing to do with it! There's a huge difference between my eating lunch with Ian and you feeding our dinner to a possum!'

'I cannert see hany difference wertsohever,' the Frog replied. He handed Anais the last fritter, and got up to go into the kitchen.

'So there's nothing for me to eat,' said Zoe, following him.

'There are serm frites left. You ave my permission to eat them erp hin the hervern hafter I ave finished cerking. Then you merst leave the kitchen himmediately.'

'Cold chips! What about my novel? I thought you cared about literature!'

'You ave pershed me too fur,' said the Frog. He began preparing the tart.

'Speaking of badly behaved wildlife, where's the Ayatollah? I don't believe he understands the verb "to share".'

'E's right nert to share is food. The cat as been taken to the vet. E's being herperated ern, to try and clean is fur. They're keeping im hovernight, hin case e as a bad reaction to the hanaesthetic.'

'We can always hope, I suppose,' said Zoe. She poured herself some wine. No one else was going to. 'I don't suppose I could try a piece of tart?'

'Nert hafter that lerst remark. This is fur the persserm, hand ernly the persserm.'

'So the possum takes precedence over me.'

'The persserm,' said the Frog with emphasis, 'did nert break hinto my secret potato cerpberd. When the tart is cerked, I will pert the frites hinto the hervern fur you, bert that is erl.'

'This whole scene has proven, once again, that you are seriously unbalanced! I can't believe the way you behave,' Zoe snapped. Snatching an apple from the fruit bowl, she went out onto the balcony and regarded the red-eyed creature sitting there. She contemplated for a moment drop-kicking it through the bougainvillea.

'I'm wertching you,' the Frog said, sticking his head out the window. A key fell from his pocket to the floor, but he didn't notice.

'So this is what I've been reduced to,' Zoe continued. 'From quails and fish with garlic croutons to a piece of suburban fruit.'

'Per'aps you'll happreciate me mere hin the future.'

The possum, believing the apple was its next course, reached up and delicately touched Zoe on the knee with its paws. 'Have it then!' she snarled. She dropped the apple on the possum's head and went back inside and started reading Antony Beevor's *Stalingrad,* exactly the right book, she thought bitterly, to prepare herself for starvation. The Soviet 65th and 21st Armies had just reached the west bank of the frozen Rossohka River, when she heard emotional farewells from the balcony. The possum must be leaving for distant parts: Siberia, she hoped.

The Frog walked into the living room a short time later. 'The chips are in the hevern, Zoe.'

She did not look up. Otherwise she would have asked the Frog why he had his hand behind his back.

'I sink I'll hiron a shirt fur termerrow, hand ave han hearly night. We ave to be ern the road first sing hin the merning, remember.'

Zoe turned the page without comment.

'Dern't furget to serlt the chips befur you heat them.'

Grimly, she kept reading—she'd be skin and bone soon—until it occurred to her that the Frog had probably never 'hironed' a shirt for the next day in his life. Zoe put down her book and tiptoed down the hall to his room.

The Frog was standing by the window, wolfing down something from a plate. The moment he saw Zoe he tried to conceal the contents. 'Leave me herlone!' he yelled, stuffing the penultimate piece of onion and cream tart into his mouth. 'Why sherd the persserm ave it erl? I wers the wern who cerked it!'

'Give me the last piece of tart!' Zoe demanded.

The Frog growled deep in his throat. 'No! It's mine!' He was red in the face and quite capable, judging from his wolfish resemblance, of doing anything required to keep her away from the plate. He had really lost it, this time. Bloody Howard, Zoe thought. He wouldn't be so casual about the Frog's mental state if he was witnessing this scene.

The phone rang and the Frog rushed down the hall. 'It might be Viola!' he cried.

'Why would it be Viola?' said Zoe through her teeth.

'Howard!' she heard the Frog say somewhat indistinctly. 'I'm so glad you pherned. Wert?...Hokay. If you sink it's a good idea. How's Zoe? She's gern quite mad. I sink you sherd terk to er.'

Zoe charged into the living room and snatched the phone from the Frog, who had the last piece of tart in his mouth. 'I want him committed! Tonight! You owe me this at least!' she shouted into the mouthpiece.

'And oo will cerk your meals?'

'He's right, you know,' said Howard. 'I think you should give things a little more time. Let's wait until after the dinner party. I promise I'll consider putting the Frog into therapy after that. In the meantime I've advised him to do some yoga to calm down. He has promised he'll begin tomorrow.'

Zoe slammed down the phone. Howard had sold his soul to the devil. After everything that had happened, she was through with both of them. Storming past the Frog, she went into the kitchen and picked up the mould of her body which was resting against the wall.

'Zoe! Dern't!' He was standing in the kitchen doorway. 'You ave no hidea ow merch I lerve your torso. Hif you destroy hit, I ham destroyed erlso!' She hesitated—remembering her plan to have her torso showcased in the window of the bookstore. In that moment, the Frog seized the mould from her, and fled. Zoe then saw the key to the deadlock lying on the floor. Grabbing it, she raced silently back to her room, and reached under her pillow for the book she had concealed there. Then she slipped out of the apartment and went down into the garden.

The thing she hadn't told the Frog—and would possibly never tell him—was that Elias Canetti's *Notes from Hampstead* was now in her possession. The second-hand book dealer she had rung the moment they returned to Sydney—an old friend—had dropped it off to her the day before. She had been reading it on the balcony after the Frog had moulded her, which was when she had come across the lines, 'He eats while sleeping, he eats when making love; walking, lying, kneeling, speaking, weeping, groaning, dying, he eats.'

Now, knowing that she was possibly deranged, she forced her way through the banana-palms in the garden. She had never, ever envisaged drowning a book until she had moved in with the Frog, but he had pushed her beyond reason.

Canetti's book sailed through the evening sky and dropped with a heavy splash into the harbour. The key followed it a second later. She sat down on the sea-wall and gazed across the water at the lights of the city. Zoe's fervent hope was that she had extinguished the Frog's literary past. She thought of those lines and shivered. *Surely* they weren't a reference to him? There was only one way to regain her literary advantage, she had to write a bestseller. It was the only solution. Perhaps then she would consider telling the Frog about the book at the bottom of the harbour. Until she had a literary past of her own, a confession was out of the question.

The Frog rose soon after sunrise on Monday morning. Zoe found him on the balcony, upside down in the bougainvillea, one leg over his head, the other out at right-angles.

'What on earth are you doing?' she asked.

'Howard terld me to do yoga!' the Frog bellowed. 'Bert I'm sterk! I cannert move! Call han hambulance!'

'I don't think there's any need to do that,' Zoe answered smoothly. 'Like Humpty Dumpty, you're about to have a great fall.'

She was right.

'I ate Dermpty Ermpty!' screamed the Frog, now on the ground. 'Stupid leetle hegg! Hand now I ave scratchers erl over my legs!' He stormed through the living room into the kitchen and splashed some water onto his face. 'I ham nevaire going to do yoga hagain! I ham mere stressed than hever! Wert a waste erf time!'

'So are we going?' Zoe asked, putting on a fedora. 'You wernted to be ern the road hearly.' She didn't notice what she had just said.

'Sterp pershing me!' he snapped. 'I ave to check we ave paprika! There his nevaire hany paprika hin this ouse!'

Zoe watched with a resigned expression as he marauded around the kitchen, opening cupboard doors and banging them shut until he found the paprika.

'Do you erlways get in serch a state when you're throwing a dinner party?' she asked.

'I ham nert hin a state! I ham erlways like this! I ham be'aving perfectly normally!'

Zoe picked up the car keys from the kitchen table. 'I'm driving,' she announced.

'Give me back my keys!' shouted the Frog.

'No, I won't. Hin the merd you're hin, you're a danger to society.'

He rounded on her, livid. 'Society is the wern who is dangerous to me! Why do you sink I ave been ferced to take erp yoga? It's erl society's ferlt!'

'I'm still driving,' said Zoe.

They argued all the way down into the street and as

they got into the car—Zoe in the driver's seat. Before she turned on the ignition, she tossed her fedora over the roll of toilet paper on the back seat.

'Why did you do that?' the Frog demanded. 'Wert appens if there's han hemergency, and I can't find the toilet paper becurse hit's idden ernder your at?'

'I'm sick of being seen in a car with toilet paper,' Zoe replied, the French accent disappearing as quickly as it had come. 'People will think we live in a caravan park.'

'I werd like to live hin a cavern perk! Maybe then I cerd get serm piss and quiet!' He sat muttering in French as they drove across Sydney and headed west towards the hills. They had left the outskirts of the city and were getting deeper into the bush when Zoe noticed they were low on petrol. At the same time, a tractor appeared out of nowhere, forcing them to slow down. 'Cretin!' the Frog yelled at the stoic figure of the driver. 'Erlways getting hin my way!' The farmer, hunched over his steering wheel, a mobile phone sticking out of the back of his pants, took no notice. With relief, Zoe saw a handwritten sign by the road just up ahead. 'We need petrol. You furgert to fill erp the tank,' she informed the Frog, and they drove into the yard and parked behind a rusty pickup truck. The accent had come back.

The house, with its old corrugated iron roof, empty beer bottles on the porch and adjoining garage with doors falling off their hinges, was more shanty dwelling than picturesque rural shack. The burnt-out wreck of a car lay just beyond the house, its tyres strewn on the ground. A barefoot man appeared from out the back, wearing a filthy pair of jeans that were sliding off his hips, and a singlet ripped across the front. He had a goatee beard and a tattoo of a snake that ran all the way down one arm.

Zoe took one look at him and turned pale. 'It might be better if you stay in the car,' she said to the Frog. 'He looks like he's on steroids. I'll do all the talking. Whatever you do, don't make any of your remarks.' She opened the car door.

'Wert remerks?' the Frog asked indignantly. 'I know ow to terk like wern erf the boys. I listen to people hin the bar.'

The owner of the shack looked Zoe up and down. 'Who are youse?' he asked.

'My name is Zoe,' she replied, without bothering to introduce the Frog, still sitting in the car.

'Yeah? I'm Leon.' He took a stubbie out of his back pocket and removed the top with his teeth. 'Pity youse aren't alone. I like chicks who run out of petrol.'

'Do you?' said Zoe weakly.

'I had a girlfriend once who looked like you.'

'Oh?' said Zoe. She looked around. 'Where is she?'

'Dunno—there's a lot of bush out there.'

Zoe heard the passenger door slam behind her. 'Bonjour,' beamed the Frog. 'Do you keep derks ern your ferm by hany chernce?'

The man narrowed his eyes. 'Speak English, mate,' he said.

'I ham speaking Hinglish. I hasked if you ad hany derks ern your ferm.'

'Ducks,' said Zoe hurriedly. 'You know, those things that quack? He's traumatised. He had a pet duck as a child, but it ran away.'

'No, I didn't,' said the Frog. 'Wert are you terking habout, Zoe?'

'Let's get the petrol, shall we?' said Zoe.

'Yeah, right,' replied the man, after another long stare at the Frog. He jerked his head towards the garage. 'The petrol's over there.' The three of them walked across the yard together.

'Wert a mervellous ole!' exclaimed the Frog, halting on the threshold of the garage and gazing with admiration at the huge pit inside. 'Is that where you keep your red wine?'

The beer-drinker took another swig. 'What are you—a wanker? It's a pit, so that you can get underneath your car and fix the fucking thing when it breaks down.'

'I nevaire know ow to fix the ferking sing,' sighed the Frog. 'When it makes a ferny noise, I send it to the mechanic. I ham bettaire hin the kitchen, although my souffle wers a ferking disaster.' He looked at Zoe proudly.

'How much do we owe you?' said Zoe, throwing the Frog a for-God's-sake-just-keep-quiet look. She paid the mechanic what he asked. 'Let's go,' she said in a low voice.

As they drove out of the dusty yard, the drinker picked up an empty beer bottle that had been lying on the ground and smashed it against the front steps of the porch.

'Wert a Nehandersal!' said the Frog. 'It's lerky you ad me with you, Zoe.'

'How far to the place where we're buying the chickens?' Zoe asked, deciding not to pursue the subject.

'Bouf! Nert far,' replied the Frog. 'The howner his a man called Watson. I rang im this merning, to horder my leetle poulets. We sherd be there hin alf han hour.'

It was, of course, much further. They reached the chicken farm after noon and drove slowly up a bumpy driveway lined with cars.

'Are you sure this is the right place?' Zoe asked. They passed a fleet of limousines covered in white streamers. 'It looks like there's a wedding going on.'

'Oui, oui, there his,' the Frog remembered. 'You were hin serch han himperssiberl merd this merning, I didn't ave a chance to tell you. Watson's daughter is getting merried.'

'How inconvenient! We can't just walk in and say we've come to collect some chickens,' groaned Zoe, as the house came into view, and then the bride and groom, posing for photographs beneath a tree.

'Herf curse we can. And we ave a glass erf champagne while we're waiting!'

'We can't,' said Zoe, appalled at his lack of protocol. 'We don't even know them!' But the Frog had bounded out of the car and was hurrying towards the wedding guests, who were milling around two long tables inside a marquee set up on the lawn. By the time she had caught up with him, the Frog had accepted a glass of champagne from a waiter, and was congratulating the bride.

'It lerks like a big der,' he said, gesturing at the scene.

'Do,' Zoe muttered in his ear. 'A big do.'

'Here's Dad now,' smiled Susan.

A huge man in a white suit stretched tight over his stomach appeared with three of his chickens wrapped up in white paper. Handing them over to the Frog, Watson chortled, 'Seen all my beauties ready for the wedding banquet?' and pointed towards the marquee, where some of his best birds, stuffed and roasted, were covered in muslin on the table, waiting to be carved.

A band started playing in the same grove of trees where the newlyweds had been posing for photographs, and all the guests in the marquee started streaming down the slope towards the music.

'I'm going to dance with Susan,' announced Watson. 'Stay and have some more champagne!' he called over his shoulder, as he and his daughter whirled away across the grass.

'I erlready ave!' the Frog shouted back.

'I think we should leave,' Zoe argued. 'I don't think I have anything in common with a chicken farmer.'

'We jerst bert three of Watson's poulets. That makes ers pert erf the family.'

'May I remind you that if we don't go now,' Zoe pointed out, 'we'll never have everything ready for tonight.'

The Frog thrust his parcels at her. 'We need han hextra chicken,' he said, and raced into the deserted marquee, returning with one of the cold roasted specimens whipped from a table.

Zoe went scarlet. If Watson or his daughter saw what the Frog had done, they'd be chicken feed—organic farm or not. 'Pert that back himmediately!' she ordered him. Still she remained oblivious to her changing accent.

'Bouf! They'll nevaire miss im. Besides, we might get angry ern the way ome. Dern't be serch a bourgeois, Zoe.'

Zoe kept silent until they were back at the car and out of earshot. 'I can't believe your behaviour! Just for doing that, you can drive!' she added, throwing the keys at him.

'I sink your ermones merst be playing erp hagain,' the Frog remarked, as he started up the engine. 'First you wernt to drive, then you dern't. Why dern't you do yoga to cerlm down, like me?'

Zoe stared out the window and said nothing. Once again, she wondered what had happened to her life—how had it gone so wrong?

'Merde!' the Frog suddenly bellowed. 'Lerk hat the time! Why did you nert remind me to lerk hat my watch?' He put his foot down on the accelerator, and they skidded out into the main road—before spinning around in a circle and coming to a screeching halt.

Zoe opened her mouth to ask what the Frog thought he was doing, then heard an odd gurgling sound. 'What's the matter?' she said in alarm. 'Are you ill?'

'Canards,' he said hoarsely.

Three plump ducks were waddling through the grass at the bottom of Watson's property.

Zoe lost her temper. 'You've erlready sterlen a chicken!' she shouted at him. 'Are you going to steal derks has well?'

'Hokay then!' the Frog shouted back. 'But you'll be serry! We cerd ave ad roast derk with prune sterffing ternight!'

'There's far too merch food erlready!' Zoe cried, feeling the madness of the previous evening beginning to sweep over her again. 'This hentire dinner perty as been hout erf cerntrel frem the stert! Oh God!' she cried, hearing the accent at last. 'Now I really know that erl his lerst!'

There was no reply from the poultry thief. The latest obstacle in his life had just appeared. Ahead was a lone cyclist dressed in racing colours, head down, bottom up, pedalling for all he was worth. 'Moron!' screamed the Frog. 'Wert's e doing hout ere hin is silly elmet? Ders e sink this his the Tour de France?'

'That's really nert fair!' exclaimed Zoe, trying desperately to keep her accent under control, as the Frog passed the cyclist on the left, leaving him in a cloud of dust. They swerved around the next corner at almost double the speed limit. The landscape had been reduced almost to a blur—trees, bush and skyline raced past like some mad slide show. She heard sirens in the distance and turned to see five police cars and a police van, blue lights flashing, coming over the crest of the hill behind them. The Frog's reaction was to drive even faster.

'You ave to sterp!' Zoe yelled at him. 'They'll harrest you hif you dern't!'

'I refuse to sterp! I do nert care habout their silly leetle sirens! They do nert make the dinner! The speed limit his nert as himpertant as my poulets hin tarragern serce!'

'I sought hit wers the poussins you cerked hin tarragern serce!' she screamed at him.

'That his nert the point!' he screamed back.

At that moment another tractor lumbered out onto the road in front of them, driven by a thin, pale man with thin, pale hair sticking out in wisps from beneath a battered brown hat.

'Merde!' bawled the Frog, slamming on the brakes. 'I ate tracters heven mere than cyclists!'

The farmer turned around and peered past Zoe and the Frog at the cavalcade fast approaching. 'Sorry,' he said. 'I didn't see you. But the police would have stopped you anyway.'

'I terld you nert to drive so fast,' Zoe moaned.

'Oh, you're French?' remarked the farmer. 'No, it's got nothing to do with breaking the speed limit. The body of a young woman was found a few hours ago. Stabbed to death. Left in the bush. Only been dead a few hours they reckon. The police are stopping everyone in the area to search their cars. I guess they thought you were suspicious, driving at such a speed.'

'How horrible,' Zoe shuddered, losing her accent in her shock. 'I knew it wasn't safe to leave the city. What can you expect when there isn't a bookstore around for miles?'

'Well, I'll tell them they dern't need to search this car,' said the Frog. 'Erl they'll find are the chickens and my grandmerther's cerking knives.'

Zoe froze. 'What did you say?'

'I said, erl they'd find are the chickens and my grandmerther's cerking knives,' the Frog repeated. 'I erlways carry them avec moi, hin case I find serm mershrerms growing hat the side erf the road.'

'Where are they?' said Zoe in a panic.

'Ernder the flap hin the boot, erl nice and cosee.'

'Quick!' cried Zoe. 'Ditch them!'

'Mais pourquoi?' said the Frog, astonished. 'They're my best cerking knives!'

It was too late. Their pursuers had pulled up alongside and, within seconds, Zoe and the Frog were surrounded by uniformed police officers, one of whom was holding a rabid alsatian on a leash.

'Is this your car, sir?' the senior officer asked.

'This his my leetle chariot, oui,' the Frog agreed. He lit a cigarette.

'A woman has been murdered. We need to search it,' the officer informed him.

'Go ahead,' the Frog replied. Two other policeman began looking in the back. Zoe flinched as one of them picked up her fedora.

'Why do you have toilet paper in your car?' queried the officer, handing the roll to his colleague to take away for fingerprinting.

'Hin case I ave to wipe my berm herf curse,' the Frog replied. 'Wert helse werd I use hit fur?'

'Three raw chickens, one cooked chicken,' said another officer, dropping them into a plastic bag. 'No croissants,' he added with a smirk. 'I thought all Frenchmen ate them.'

'I dern't heat croissants,' the Frog corrected him.

'They make my stermach rermble like a leetle hengine-houtberd. And leave my chickens herlone. They're fur the dinner perty we're aving ternight.'

'Too bad. Boot,' said the senior officer, taking the keys from the ignition, and passing them to one of his men.

'It smells like gherkins in here,' the policeman commented, poking around gingerly in the interior. He passed a tea towel covered in red blotches to the dog-handler.

'Wine stains,' the dog-handler pronounced. The dog, in its excitement, ripped the tea towel to pieces. 'Some idiot poured red wine into Matey's water bowl once, and he never got over the experience.'

'What's under there?' continued the sharp-eyed senior officer, pointing at the side-flap.

'Oh no,' Zoe gasped. 'This is a nightmare.' She clutched the Frog's arm, her heart racing. 'When you go to jail, I'll have to learn to cook.' Jokes had never been her strong point.

The policeman triumphantly held up the knives and a bell began tolling in the distance.

'Why is there always a bell tolling somewhere?' Zoe croaked. 'Is it a sign from Proust? Should I put a bell in my novel?'

'That's just my wife, letting me know that lunch is ready,' said the farmer, looking at her with puzzled eyes.

One minute she was French, the next minute she wasn't.

'Wert are you aving?' the Frog asked with interest. 'Ders your wife make leek soup?'

'Steak and kidney pie, as far as I know,' said the farmer.

The Frog looked wistful. 'Can Zoe and I cerm too?'

'You're not going anywhere,' said the senior policeman, signalling one of his men to bring the handcuffs. 'Could be we just found our murder weapon.'

'Wert's the mattaire?' barked the Frog. 'Those are my grandmerther's cerking knives. She left them to me hin er will. Hit's very himpertant to ave good cerking knives. Hanglo-Saxons ave no idea. These werns are very special to me. I nevaire leave ome without them.'

'Really,' said the senior officer. 'Can you tell us why you keep them hidden behind the flap?'

'They're nert idden—I dern't want them to get rersty,' the Frog contradicted him. 'And I keep them hin the car hin case I see serm mershrerms hin the forest. You nevaire know when you might break down, or rern hout erf petrol. We ave erlready rern hout erf petrol wernce today. We might ave ad to skin han heel, or dig hin the ground for a potato hin horder to survive.'

'Anyone would think you lived in a cave,' the officer remarked, snapping the handcuffs on the Frog's wrists.

'I *sherd* live hin a cave! I erlways wanted to live hin a cave! Maybe then people werd sterp hinterfering hin my life! Why ave you pert andcerffs ern me?'

'You're under arrest,' the senior officer replied. 'And your companion is coming with us as well,' he added, with a grim look at Zoe. 'I'm taking you both back to headquarters for further questioning. Move that tractor,' he ordered the farmer. 'You're blocking the road.'

'This his han houtrage!' choked the Frog. 'Ow dare you harrest me? Wert ave I dern?'

'You've got the wrong man,' said Zoe in desperation. 'I know who the murderer must be. We bought petrol from him earlier on. His name is Leon, and he lives in this awful house with beer bottles, and he's got a tattoo of a snake down one arm.'

'Oh, Leon,' said the officer. 'Why try to put the blame on him? Leon's no murderer. He's a famous artist—our local Jackson Pollock. His work hangs in the National Gallery. Next to Pollock's as a matter of fact. I'm surprised you didn't recognise him. He does the arts program on TV.'

He led her over to another police car next to the one where the Frog was now sitting between two junior policemen, and opened the door. 'Mind your head.'

In despair, Zoe got in, twisting around towards the other prisoner just as he managed to lean across his escorts and bellow out the window at her, 'Himbeciles! I ham cursed hin this life, cursed! We merst hescape to Guadeloupe! Thus his the ernly solution!' A policeman handed the Frog's car keys to a colleague.

'Of course—that's it!' thought Zoe, as they headed off, sirens screaming, back towards the city. 'A famous artist working on the new *Blue Poles*, goes bush for inspiration, cracks under the strain of isolation, gets a tattoo like the locals and murders a farmer's wife.'

At last, after all this time on her long, hard literary journey, she had her plot.

'Tell me again about the knives in your car.'

'I've terld you wern erndred times!' bawled the Frog. 'Why dern't you get han earing haid, you silly trout?'

'Now is not the time to try out your English expressions,' Zoe hinted from across the interview room. Her face was showing the strain. They were in serious trouble and there was no point making the situation worse with a display of French attitude. The three policemen in charge of the interrogation remained blank-faced.

'Tell me again,' said one.

'Non! Je refuse!'

The door of the interview room opened and Zoe, who

had been wondering when they would formally be charged with murder, fixed her eyes on the tall, elegant policeman in plainclothes who had just entered. He bore a small but unmistakable resemblance to Mikhail Bulgakov.

'Good afternoon,' he said, although it was almost five o'clock. 'I'm Chief Inspector Antoine Quill.' He glanced at Zoe and then at the Frog.

'You're French?' cried the Frog. 'Thank God!' For once, Zoe could only agree with him.

'Only a quarter,' said Quill. 'On my mother's side.'

'Bouf! Furget habout the quarter! French blerd takes precedence hover hany erther sert,' the Frog enthused.

The interrogating officer stood up. 'It's hopeless, Chief Inspector,' he said. 'He won't confess. He's sticking to his story about the wild mushrooms. And he keeps demanding his chickens back.'

'Tell me,' the chief inspector said to the Frog. 'How do you make mushroom soup?'

'Why do you wernt to know?'

'Humour me.'

'Well, to be ernest, I werd rerther pert wild mershrerms hin han homolette,' barked the Frog. 'But since you hinsist ern pertting them hin the soup, you will need, earlier, to ave made a good veal or chicken sterk. That's fur hadded flavour. Then you rinse the mershrerms hin cold werter, and wipe them dry. Get rid erf hany dirt ern them avec a clerth. The clerth can be a leetle damp. Do nert rerb them like han hidiot! Mershrerms are very delicate! You merst peel them or remove the stalks. Cut them so!' he made a chopping motion with his hand, and all the policemen in the room leaned forward. 'Then cerk them hin melted buttaire hin a sercepan erntil they are soft. Had a leetle cherpped garlic, serm cherpped parsley, salt and pepper, grated nertmeg and keep cerking a leetle lernger.'

He broke off as the door opened again and a fifth policeman walked in with the cold roast chicken which the Frog had stolen from the wedding.

'Lernch!' cried the Frog, overjoyed. 'We aven't ad erny yet!'

'Let's return to the soup for a minute,' said Chief Inspector Quill. 'I think there's something you still need to add.'

'Has husual, I ave to tell people heverysing!' snapped the Frog, his eyes glued to the roast chicken. 'You sherd ave been soaking a slice erf white bread hin serm erf the sterk. Make sure you cert erff the crerst. Then wring hout the moisture and hadd the bread to the mershrerms. Keep cerking. Then you ave to pert heverysing through a mouli—do I ave to go ern?'

'No, no,' said Quill. 'That's how my mother used to make mushroom soup as well. Just one more thing. I want you to demonstrate how to carve a chicken.'

'Herf curse, with pleasure!' said the Frog. 'Werd you like a breast or a wing?'

'Just carve.'

As the chicken was placed in front of him, an officer rather reluctantly handed the Frog one of the suspected murder weapons and a carving fork.

'Wertch careferlly!' the Frog instructed everyone in the room, as he took the knife in his right hand. 'I dern't wernt to ave to show you hagain.' A split second later, like a conjurer performing a magic trick, he held up a thin, beautifully carved slice of white meat. The change of atmosphere in the interview room was palpable.

'Bravo!' applauded Quill, and even the interrogating officers smiled. 'Can I have a go?' Taking the knife, he plunged it into the bird.

'Nert like that!' the Frog screamed in anguish. 'Mon Dieu! Wert a massacre! You're has bad has Zoe! You sherd ave seen the carnage the night I cerked er quails! Give me the knife. You sink it his Hexcalibur?'

'Sorry,' muttered Quill. 'I never did learn how to carve properly. Still, it probably doesn't matter when you live on takeaway chicken like I do.'

'Houtrageous!' exclaimed the Frog. 'Ow can you be French and heat takehaway? You ad bettaire come to hour dinner perty tonight. There you will taste real food. Height ho'clock! Dern't be late!'

'It's almost six already,' said Quill, glancing at his

watch. 'I'll give you a police escort home.'

'You mean we're free?' gasped Zoe, not quite believing it. She felt like embracing him, and asking him his views on Maigret. 'How can you be sure the Frog is innocent? I mean, not that I want him to go to jail—sincerely, I don't want that to happen—but he is pretty strange. Even without the knives, I can understand why you arrested him.'

'The moment he carved the chicken, we knew he wasn't our man,' Quill answered. 'The killer used his left hand to stab his victim. We've got another suspect in custody. We're pretty sure it's him.'

'The cyclist!' pronounced the Frog. 'I knew it! Cyclists are erl criminerls. Ave you seen the way they treat the road has hif they howned it?'

Quill shook his head. 'Not a cyclist,' he said. 'A farmer. Stoic type. Carrying a mobile. Sat on his tractor and refused to let a police car pass. That was his downfall. Our officers found spots of bloods on his clothes after they took him in for questioning.' He paused. 'There is, of course, the matter of a stolen chicken. We've had a complaint from a wedding guest who says he witnessed a snatch and grab earlier on today. In the interests of cooking time, though, I think we'll tell him it must be a case of mistaken identity.'

The peak-hour traffic was no match for the police escort. But even the added glamour of two out-riders following behind as they raced across the harbour bridge failed to distract Zoe. 'I was sure the murderer was the man on the shanty farm. He practically admitted he had buried his girlfriend in the bush,' she said in a disgruntled voice.

The Frog was so thrilled by the sight of traffic giving way left, right and centre, that he took no notice of what she was saying. 'I sherd erlways ave a per-leece hescert!' he bellowed. 'This his the ernly way to drive!'

'So you don't want to escape to Guadeloupe any more?'

'Nert right now. I have to cerk.'

They arrived at the apartment and the Frog rushed up the stairs with all his chickens under one arm. 'We merst erry!' he called over his shoulder to Zoe. 'There his no time to lerse!'

'I'll help you,' said Zoe, once they were in the kitchen. She watched with dismay as the Frog started juggling pots, pans, poussins, chickens, quails and a trout.

'Non! Will you nevaire learn? I dern't wernt you hin the kitchen!' the Frog shouted, pulling the pigs' trotters out of the fridge and spilling the leeks all over the floor. 'Where's the cheese? It merst stert breathing! And where's the hoil? Jerst has well the door to the secret potato cupberd his broken, becurse I cannert find the key!'

Zoe, who had turned to flee the moment she saw the pigs' trotters, realised the awful truth as the Frog pushed her out of the kitchen and deadlocked the door behind her. She had thrown the wrong key into the harbour.

At eight o'clock, on the dot, the guests arrived at the door en masse—Max and Madeleine, dressed (bless them, thought Zoe) in black tie; Russell, in a red silk designer artist's smock which made him look ridiculous; Louise, in a Max Mara outfit; the Fitzwimpletons, in clothes you'd wear to go boating on a rainy day; Eva, in a tight crocodile-skin dress; Howard, in jeans, a zebra-print belt and a dinner jacket; Antarctica in an anorak worn over a sweeping evening gown; Ian, in erudite black velvet; and Chief Inspector Antoine Quill, resplendent in a kilt. 'My grandfather was Scottish,' he explained to Zoe, who was wearing her Vargas Llosa catsuit. Just in case.

'Do come in,' she said, ushering everyone inside.

'We left the children with a babysitter. We thought that would be safer,' said the Fitzwimpletons, their eyes darting around the living room. 'How quaint,' Judith added, scanning the bookshelves, the portrait of Bonaparte and the Brassai photograph. 'You obviously don't have a decorator. Tell me, do you always have such a huge French flag hanging over the dinner table?'

'Sermtimes we use it has a berth towel,' said Zoe. She

put a hand to her forehead. Oh God, it was happening again. 'Why...don't...we...go...out...ern, merde!...the balcony?' she suggested, trying to look at ease.

'Wouldn't it be nice if there were penguins in the harbour,' said Antarctica wistfully, as the guests lined the balcony railing, gazing at the view. Howard patted her bottom in a comforting manner and gestured at the torn and broken bougainvillea. 'What happened?' he asked.

'The Frog was doing yoga,' Zoe answered. 'Just like you suggested. He confused the lotus position.' Her tone was cool. She hadn't forgiven Howard for siding with the Frog over the drugging and kidnapping episode.

'Where *is* the host?' asked Ian. 'I've heard so much about him. He sounds exactly like the rich, vibrant, larger-than-life character publishers like to meet.'

Too late, Zoe remembered she had forgotten to close the kitchen window.

'I ate this sercepan! Hit tries to destroy heverysing I do! My life his a sheet!' a voice bellowed on cue.

'Well, really!' said Judith Fitzwimpleton. 'Can't he swear in French?'

The saucepan just missed her. It sailed across the tree fern, almost hitting the Ayatollah, who had taken up his usual surveillance position amidst the fronds. The cat vanished into the banana-palms. 'Such fun,' said Madeleine.

Donald Fitzwimpleton turned to Chief Inspector Quill. 'I understand you're a policeman,' he said. 'Tell me—how did you meet our host?'

'He was taken into custody this afternoon as a murder suspect,' Quill replied.

'I knew it!' exclaimed Judith Fitzwimpleton. 'Thank God we didn't bring the children!'

'The Frog his hinnocernt,' said Zoe. 'It wers erl a mix-up.'

'I doubt that very much,' Judith replied. 'You know, you're speaking in a very strange fashion. Have you been staying up too late writing your novel? What an effort—and for what? I mean, do people *read* novels any more? I prefer glossy magazines.'

'As Alberto Moravia once said, "The ratio of literacy to illiteracy is constant, but nowadays the illiterates can read,"' quoted Zoe, her voice trembling slightly, but otherwise managing to keep her accent straight.

'Well said!' Ian concurred.

'Merde!' came another bellow from the kitchen. 'I ave a terriberl pain! I sink I ham dying!'

'Take no notice. He's probably just eaten one of the main courses,' Zoe reassured everyone.

'Oh look!' cried Antarctica, who had just spotted the scarecrow. 'An art installation!'

'For Christ's sake!' said Russell. He smoothed down his smock and tried to remain calm. After all, he was an Archibald Prize winner. 'Any chance of a drink, Zoe?'

'Yes, of course,' said Zoe, more confidently than she felt. She walked back inside and hammered on the kitchen door. 'Open up! Our guests are here! I have to get the champagne from the fridge!'

'Tell them to go haway! I'm nert ready yet!'

Eva appeared. 'Typical French,' she said to Zoe. 'They feel so besieged by the European Union, they have to lock themselves in their kitchens.'

The door swung open. The Frog stood there in the same pair of jeans and blue shirt he had been wearing all day, a soup stain on his collar and lentils sticking to his chin. 'I eard that!' he shouted. 'It's nert the Huropean Union I ham trying to havoid hin ere, it's umanity! Why can't people be mere like salmern?'

'What do you mean?' asked Howard, coming from the balcony with the others. 'You'd like to be a fish?' He shot a significant look at Zoe, who ignored him.

'Salmern die hafter reproderktion! That's wert mankind sherd do! Ernly then werd the world becerm a bettaire place, and I cerd get serm piss hand quiet!'

'Isn't that rather an extreme view?' asked Donald Fitzwimpleton. 'Why do you think we have downsizing?'

'Herpsizing, dernsizing, hit's herl the same to me!' bellowed the Frog. 'We sherd sterp perpulating the planet this minute!'

'But then mankind would die out,' said Antarctica sadly.

'That's precisely the point! Do you sink I henjoy wertching the meals I make, being mutilated by fureigners?'

Max and Madeleine grinned, but there was muttering from everyone else. Even Quill looked a bit put out.

'I'll get the champagne,' said Zoe, before things turned ugly. 'Shall we go back out to the balcony and have it there?'

'No! There hisn't henerf time! Heverywern merst sit down hat the table now.' bawled the Frog. 'They can drink their champagne with the first curse. Hif we dern't stert heating now, we'll be ere erl night.' He herded everyone back into the living room. 'The first curse his leek soup.' he continued. 'Then fish soup with garlic croutons, and my brilliant terrine. Main curses—pay hattention—poussins hin tarragern serce, trout avec mayhonnaise, coq au vin, rabbit hin red wine, lentils with Italian sersages, and Singapore noddles, cerked hin my new wok. Vegetaberls—potatoes hin goose fat and puree erf broad beans. Then fromage. Then—the big surprise!'

Moving to the table, he stood to attention beneath the French flag. 'Pigs' trertters coated with breadcrembs and served with a serce tartare!'

There was utter and complete silence, save for Antarctica asking Howard in a stage whisper, 'Can you get fluid retention from pigs' trotters?'

'No dessert then,' said Max, trying to inject a note of comedy into the proceedings.

'Herf curse there's dessert!' roared the Frog. 'Creme caramel and erm—' He broke off abruptly.

'What?' said Louise curiously.

'Wait and see,' said the Frog.

The doorbell rang.

'Is this the right address?' Viola asked, hitching up her fishnet stockings and undoing the only button that more or less closed the flimsy crimson dress she was wearing.

Zoe froze as the novelist-prostitute strode past her down the hall. Spiky hair dyed bright red, nails dangerously long, new stilettos gleaming, she paused dramatically in the living-room doorway, before sashaying over to the table and sliding into the empty seat next to Ian.

'Viola!' cried the Frog in delight. 'Have you met everyone?'

'I know Antoine,' Viola answered, who had just spotted him.

'Nice to see you, Viola,' Quill replied. 'Long time, no see. How's the profit margin?'

'No arguments from the shareholders,' Viola replied.

'You don't work with Max, do you?' said Louise uncertainly.

'Who?' Viola asked.

'What business are you in?' Judith asked in a clipped manner.

'Hydraulics,' said Viola. 'Keeps me busy. Never a dull moment—eh, Antoine?'

'Why did you invite her?' Zoe hissed under her breath, as the Frog continued to beam like an idiot at his tardy guest. 'She looks like a vampire in that outfit!' Viola picked up the bottle of Saltram Barossa Shiraz 1994 which Zoe had just opened and took a swig.

'The problem is,' said Viola, addressing the table, 'I'm not getting enough time to write.'

'What?' said Ian, instantly intrigued. 'Tell me more.'

'My book,' said Viola. '*The Riddle of the Ripped G-String.*'

'We must have lunch!' Ian exclaimed, pulling out a diary from his trouser pocket. 'Are you free tomorrow?'

Zoe slid over and stabbed him in the arm with a fingernail. 'You're not serious,' she hissed in his ear. 'She's writing a sordid little novel about sex!'

'Marvellous,' replied her publisher.

The Frog, who had again disappeared into the kitchen, now rushed back into the room like a whirlwind, stained tea towel tied around his neck, balancing an extraordinary pile of dishes in his arms. 'Now that Viola is ere, we can heat!' he announced, sliding plates onto the table. 'Leek soup first! Then the feesh! Then terrine! Then the poussins and the trout! Erry erp, befur the coq au vin goes cerld. There's no time fur the sersages and lentils—besides, I've herlready heaten them. And the Singapore noddles get sterk to the wok. I knew I sherd ave stir-fried them hin goose fat. Now I ave to go berk and pert the rabbit, the pigs' trertters and the creme caramel hin the hervern. There wersn't hany room before.'

Zoe pushed back her chair and hurried after him into the kitchen. 'Gid rid of those pigs' trotters at once! I won't have them served! You can't! How can you do this to me—a writer?'

'Get hout erf my kitchen!'

'And you can't serve all these dishes at once! This is ridiculous!'

'Hout erf my way!' bellowed the Frog. 'Go and lerk hafter hour guests!'

'I suppose I'll have to try some of this leek soup stuff after all,' Viola was commenting, as Zoe, in total despair, sat down opposite the prostitute. 'In my line of work, you lose your appetite half the time.'

'You poor thing,' snapped Zoe. 'And it's not so safe sucking blood any more either, is it?'

The Frog came back in, beaming. 'Heverysing his cerking merrily haway hin the hevern,' he announced. 'What do you sink erf the soup, Viola?'

'Jeez,' said Viola, taking a mouthful of the soup. 'Makes a nice change after swallowing—'

'Don't you dare!' interrupted Zoe. 'I'm warning you!'

Howard reached over and put a restraining hand on

her arm. 'Go with the flow, Zoe,' he told her. 'Viola's only expressing herself.'

Zoe fled to the kitchen to recover her composure. 'Of course, Donald and I prefer postmodern food, but it's true this leek soup has a certain style,' remarked Judith Fitzwimpleton.

'Try the fish soup,' said Madeleine. 'It's sublime.'

'This terrine is heaven,' garbled Antarctica. 'There's no penguin meat in it, is there?'

'Next time!' promised the Frog, sitting down next to her.

'Sorry trout,' apologised Antarctica, 'but I don't think fish have feelings.' She added in a worried tone, 'Except when they get caught on a hook, I suppose.'

'Mais non,' said the Frog. 'Feesh die hin their sleep.' He shovelled most of the potatoes in goose fat onto his plate.

'I'd get some poussins now if I was you,' Louise suggested to Russell, whose head had begun to spin at the sight of everyone clambering for different dishes.

'Watch out!' shouted Max, as the puree of broad beans tipped over.

'That's why we wore wet weather gear,' Judith Fitzwimpleton explained to Zoe, who had rejoined the table.

'We can mop it up with the bread,' said Viola efficiently, tearing a baguette to bits.

'Do you think I could have just one potato in goose fat?' Donald Fitzwimpleton demanded.

'Too late!' cried the Frog. 'You erlways manage to miss hout, dern't you!'

'What's the secret of great cooking?' Howard inquired, grabbing the coq au vin from Antoine Quill while Donald Fitzwimpleton filched Ian's trout when he wasn't looking.

'The secret his to be angry,' the Frog replied imperiously.

'So in view of the marvellous atmosphere around this dinner table tonight,' continued Howard, 'don't you feel, despite everything, that there's an art to living after all?'

'The hart erf living his the ernly hexcuse to go ern living,' the Frog corrected him, raising his wineglass to his lips.

PHOOM! A huge explosion came from the kitchen. It caused the French flag to crash onto the table, breaking dishes and draping everyone in its blue, red and white folds.

'It's not Bastille Day, is it?' said a muffled voice from somewhere.

'My pigs' trertters!' Everyone's blood froze at the Frog's terrible cry. Throwing off the flag, their host raced into the kitchen. First, there was silence, and then came a howl of such suffering that the Ayatollah, still sitting in the tree fern, cowered behind the fronds.

'A criminerl as sabotaged my hevern! Heverysing his destroyed! Quelle catastrophe!'

There was the sound of chairs scraping, and then all the guests appeared in the kitchen doorway, craning their necks to see the Frog sitting amid the ruins of dinner, repeating, 'I ham cursed hin this life,' like a mantra. Splattered on the walls around him were the remains of the pigs' trotters, the rabbit, and eleven creme caramels.

'The temperature wers turned erp to the maximum,' the Frog said in a heartbroken voice. 'Who werd do serch a sing?'

Everyone bowed their heads. No one knew what to say. Except Zoe. 'It must have been the Ayatollah.'

'I ham nevaire, hever, cerking hagain. My art his broken,' wept the Frog. 'I ave lerst erl ope. I ham ernly glad my grandmerther his nert halive to see this.'

Madeleine knelt down beside him. 'All is not lost,' she reminded her husband's best friend. 'You said there was another dessert, remember? A surprise.'

'That's right,' said the Frog, his tear-stained face brightening. 'Ow cerd I ave furgertten?' Getting shakily to his feet, he threw open the door of the fridge. 'White chocolate mousse!' he shouted.

The evening roared back into life. More wine was opened, and champagne, and the Frog was carried back into the living room on the shoulders of the male guests—even Donald Fitzwimpleton lent a hand—bearing aloft the white chocolate mousse in a glittering crystal bowl.

As someone turned up Jacques Brel to full volume, Louise removed the broken dishes from the table. 'What shall I do with these?' she asked the Frog, who was stalking Zoe with a serving of the mousse.

'Throw em hin the arbour!' he bellowed.

The Ayatollah, taking advantage of all the pandemonium, sprang into the kitchen and started licking the creme caramels off the wall.

'Do you do S&M?' Howard asked Viola.

Judith Fitzwimpleton ate a spoonful of the mousse and flushed bright pink. Behind her husband's back, she started pawing Antoine Quill's kilt.

Zoe took her serving from the Frog without thinking and soon after experienced the most peculiar tingling in her spine, which began to spread throughout her body. As she gave little gasps of pleasure, her vision began to blur to such an extent that she could hardly see the other guests. Only the Frog, bigger and brighter than ever, glowed like a—like a—'Darling,' Zoe purred, unzipping her catsuit and letting it slide off her shoulders. 'Your mousse is wonderful. Can I have some more?'

The Frog grabbed Judith Fitzwimpleton's dessert bowl. 'Ave erl erf hit!' he shouted, spooning it into Zoe's mouth.

Max and Madeleine danced past them to salsa music, Donald and Viola disappeared through the front door, and Ian took the Frog aside and began an urgent conversation.

By the time Zoe found the energy to wipe the mousse off her mouth, the living room was completely empty except for the Frog. With a tea towel hanging lecherously off one shoulder, he was circling her with intent.

'Wait,' she said brokenly. 'I'm not an iguana.'

'Cerm to me!' breathed the Frog, stubbing out his cigarette. 'I premerise I'll give erp smerking.'

Somewhere in Zoe's brain, a tiny, lost alarm bell rang. God, what was it the Frog had told her about white chocolate mousse? She peered at him again. He had become unbearably attractive. Even his tea towel seemed romantic. How could this be?

'Wait,' she said, trying to wave him away. 'Let's not rush it. I can't be distracted from my book.'

'We ave to rersh hit!' shouted the Frog, pulling off his cardinal socks and unzipping his trousers. 'I've got a book to write now too!'

'Wert?' said Zoe, in shock. 'Wert are you terking habout?'

'Yarn as signed me to a cerntract,' the Frog said importantly. 'I ham going to write a berk cerlled *Jerstice fur Radishes*. Yarn says the ernly berks that sell these days are habout food and sex.'

Zoe stared at him. 'Bert wert habout my berk?' she stammered.

'Yarn says you ave a lert erf werk to do ern hit. You're speaking with a French haccent, Zoe.'

She didn't hear. She was dazed. What if *Justice for Radishes* outsold her own plot-muddled, untitled work? Zoe thought of Bertolt Brecht: 'Literature has the right and the duty to give to the public the ideas of the time.' Radishes had been around for ages. Who cared about them anyway?

'You can't do this to me,' she said in a small voice. 'I'm meant to be the writer hin this relationship. You're meant to do the cerking. I sought that wers the deal. Ow ham I going to heat, hif we're both writing berks?'

'Sings will ave to change haround ere,' the Frog replied.

'Ow will *you* heat?' Zoe said suddenly. 'I can't cerk, remember?' It was her only card. She held her breath. The Ayatollah came in, chewing on bits of rabbit, but the Frog and Zoe had eyes only for each other.

'I adn't sought er that,' the Frog admitted. 'Wert shall I do?'

Zoe pulled the catsuit right off. Then she removed her underwear and dangled it invitingly over volume one of Proust.

'The sing his,' she said, 'I've jerst remembered that sex makes me write twice as fast.'

'So,' the Frog said hoarsely, 'once you finished yours, I cerd write mine?'

'Sermsing like that.'

'Do you mind getting ern the table? I erlways wernted to make lerve ern terp erf the French flag.'

'Hif we merst.'

'Werd you like a gherkin befur we begin?'

'Hokay—that werd be nice.'

'I ope you dern't mind the damp spert frem the puree of broad beans.'

'Nert at erl. Tell me—wert wers really hin the white chocolate mousse?'

'Triple martinis. I like your hunderwear anging hover Proust. His Proust really your favourite horser?'

'I'm nert really sure. I've nevaire hactually read im. His that a lentil ern your, um?' Zoe asked.

'Lentils are so nerty!' replied the Frog, as the Ayatollah slunk from the room. 'Zoe?'

'Mmmmm?'

'Do you sink that wern day, you cerd *try* to heat serm pigs' trertters?'

ACKNOWLEDGMENTS

Thanks to my family and friends for tolerating my absences and my moods while I was writing; to my publisher Michael Heyward, who saw the potential of *Monsieur Frog* and acquired a French accent along the way—for his patience, his wit and his vision for the novel; to Melanie Ostell, for her excellent editing, and to Emily Booth and Donica Bettanin for their calming influence; to Rose Creswell and Jane Cameron, for keeping me on the straight and narrow in the early stages of writing; and to my *Good Weekend* colleagues who so warmly embraced 'the Frog' when he first leaped into print as an irregular column.